DARK SECRET

After the tragic loss of her father and brothers at sea, Emily couldn't provide for the rest of the family by continuing the family tradition of fishing as her father's boat had been lost in the accident and he hadn't kept up the insurance payments on it. So, the family moved to relatives in Plymouth. Emily obtained a position as housemaid at Mountford Hall — though she could never have foreseen what fate had in store for her when she took up her new post . . .

*Books by Joyce Johnson
in the Linford Romance Library:*

ROUGH MAGIC
BITTER LEGACY
HOSTAGES OF FATE
SWEET LEGACY

JOYCE JOHNSON

DARK SECRET

Complete and Unabridged

LINFORD
Leicester

First published in Great Britain

First Linford Edition
published 2000

British Library CIP Data

ROM
1349890

Johnson, Joyce, *1931 –*
Dark secret.—Large print ed.—
Linford romance library
1. Love stories
2. Large type books
I. Title
813.5′4 [F]

ISBN 0–7089–5730–7

Published by
F. A. Thorpe (Publishing)
Anstey, Leicestershire

Set by Words & Graphics Ltd.
Anstey, Leicestershire
Printed and bound in Great Britain by
T. J. International Ltd., Padstow, Cornwall

This book is printed on acid-free paper

1

Emily Trembarth tightened her grip on her mother's shoulder as the dreadful litany rang mournfully on the still summer air: 'Jack Pascoe . . . Adam Pascoe . . . Samuel Rosevear . . . ' The young minister's voice faltered — Sam, his own well-loved uncle! 'Benjamin Rosevear . . . ' — his young cousin, out on his first fishing trip, hardly grown to boyhood. He prayed for the strength to continue. 'George Trembarth, John and Matthew Trembarth, sons to George and Sarah . . . '

Emily felt her mother's body shudder, saw her glance behind to Aunt Maud and Uncle Will as if drawing strength from their presence, as well as from that of her two daughters.

Tiny Polly Trembarth clutched her sister's skirt. Not yet five years old, she wasn't sure what they were all doing,

1

standing so solemn and sad out on the cliff top in the hot sun. Usually such a day meant a picnic on the rocks with Emily, looking for shrimps. But there'd not been a single picnic since that day Dad and John and Matt hadn't come back from the fishing.

Lots of other dads and brothers hadn't come back either — and nothing in the village had been the same again. She missed her big daddy and brothers swinging her up on their shoulders, telling her she was a little feather compared to the baskets of fish they'd hauled up the quay. Now no-one laughed in the village any more, especially not Mum and Emily. Polly's lower lip quivered and before Emily could reach down, her sobs were all but drowning out the roll call of Treskillen's many dead.

Choking back her own grief, Emily swiftly kneeled to comfort her small sister. Poor little Polly — her childhood snatched away by a capricious Cornish spring storm a month ago.

'Hush, it won't be long now. Reverend Rosevear's going to bless the cross by the cliff edge with Daddy's name — and Matt's, and John's. We'll look in a minute or so, then we'll go home.'

She stood up, but kept her sister close to her. In spite of the hot sun, Emily shivered and pulled her shawl tight round her shoulders. She gazed out to sea. That blue calm — hardly a ripple — deceitful, treacherous. Yet she couldn't condemn it. The sea was part of her — in her heart and blood.

She was a Trembarth, and Trembarths had lived by the sea in Treskillen for centuries. It had given most of the folk of Treskillen a living, sometimes generously, sometimes grudgingly, but on that one fateful day in the first decade of the twentieth century, it had extracted fearful payment from the village.

That payment day had started two months earlier with just such a smiling face as today. A beguiling sea, merely ruffled by a spring breeze, had lulled

Treskillen's fishing boats out on the dawn tide promising fair weather and a fat catch of fish. But for a sprained ankle, Emily would have sailed with them. As it was, she had waved the boats out of sight round the headland, then hobbled painfully back to the family's cottage halfway up the hill from the harbour. It was one of the rare occasions she'd missed a sailing since she'd left the village school four years earlier.

A stronger wind had blown up during the morning, but the women of Treskillen carried out their household chores as usual. Their men were experienced, their boats sturdy. Out there, way beyond the harbour, the fishermen filled their nets and looked forward to an extra pint in The Fisherman's Rest that night. Nothing could have prepared them for the sudden vicious squall that sprang up as the tide changed.

As they turned homewards to run before the wind, driving rain and thick mists reduced visibility to zero. One boat veered wildly off course, slammed into its neighbour, and a third was thrown into the locked vessels.

Bill Pearn, one of the few survivors, told his tale over and over as though he could never be rid of it.

' 'Twas like the Lord himself was enraged, and picked up the entire fleet like babby's boats and flung us in temper in a tangled mess.'

Bill was to spend the rest of his life wondering why he had survived when so many had drowned.

Emily kneeled at the minister's request, along with the rest of the congregation, and the simple memorial service ended with the familiar prayer for seamen throughout the world.

The bereaved families lingered on the cliff top, reluctant to leave, almost as though it would be an affront to the spirits of their dead to leave them and go back to their lonely homes. Small knots of people clustered around the granite pillar.

5

The minister moved among them, desperately dredging up words of appropriate comfort. He paused by the Trembarths.

'Mrs Trembarth, your George and the boys were fine men. Emily, you'll be looking out for your mother now, and Polly, too.'

He patted the child's dark head and looked questioningly at the older couple standing sentinel by Sarah Trembarth.

The man, thick set, balding, stepped forward, hand held out.

'Minister, I'm Will Broome, from Plymouth, and this is my wife Maud, Sarah's elder sister. We've come to see to things here, now Mrs Trembarth's men have gone.'

'Good of you to come so far.'

'We're Sarah's family. Families must stick together.'

Maud, a strong-looking, handsome grey-haired woman, nodded to the minister as she took her sister's arm.

'Come along now, Sarah. It's time to go. We haven't got long. Emily, you'll follow right on, with Polly.'

'I just want to talk to Harry . . . Harry Rosevear. He lost his dad and brother. They . . . they're still out in the bay. His mother's taken it hard . . . no bodies, you see.'

Will Broome shook his head. 'Such tragedy. A sad day for everyone.'

'The death of Treskillen,' Sarah Trembarth flung out.

George Trembarth and his ancestors had been accustomed to the harshness of the fickle sea, and had philosophically accepted that the family tree's roots and branches were scarred with the black crosses of premature death by drowning. But Sarah Penrose had come from the next county, Devon, of farming folk, and had never quite accepted her husband's seafaring way of life.

The anxiety of every storm, fear every time the maroons fired in distress, the deaths, the mourning — and the gaps. Now at least it was ended. There were no more male Trembarths at Treskillen.

7

George's brothers had emigrated to America when the tin had run out of the local mines; cousins and second cousins had carried on farming, or working at the great Mountford Estate — an estate engulfing acre on acre across Southern Cornwall, and which included Treskillen village.

'We're finished here,' Sarah said dully, 'there's nothing for us — nothing to keep us.'

'Mother! Don't say that,' Emily cried, 'we three are still here. It's where we belong. There's plenty folk left in the village . . . our friends'll help.'

'I've done with it.'

Sarah began to weep, and her daughter's heart turned to ice. This is what she'd feared — in all the weeks since the drownings, but had never dared to talk about, fearful of what she'd hear. Since the storm which had taken her men, Sarah Trembarth had been frozen in limbo. Now, after the memorial service, the symbolic farewell, she could begin to thaw — and that's when her pain started.

Unlike Emily, she found it impossible even to look at the sea. She wanted to get away, start afresh. She turned to her sister, and wept against her broad shoulder.

'Come now, Sarah, we'll go home. You must eat something, then we'll talk. Emily, I want you back at the cottage. Your young man can wait.'

'He's not my young man. He's just my friend!'

Emily bit back a sharper retort. Harry Rosevear, son of a deep-rooted Treskillen family, had been her ally and companion ever since they'd shared the same battle-scarred wooden desk in the village school. They'd played in the woods beyond the harbour, swum, sailed and fished together. Life without Harry was difficult to imagine. She tossed a defiant look at her stern-faced aunt. Why had she come back to Treskillen again?

Aunt Maud and Uncle Will had been to the lavish and sombre public funeral weeks ago. It had been the first and only time Maud Penrose had set foot in Treskillen. She had her private reasons for hating the place but neither had she ever approved the radically independent and outspoken George Trembarth, considering him feckless and unreliable.

What had happened was no more than she'd always expected. She narrowed her eyes now at her niece — that stubborn Trembarth streak, just like her father. She'd spotted it at the funeral, but there'd been no time for action then — there'd been too many folk around.

The Treskillen tragedy had caught the nation's imagination. Newspaper men even came from London, and the Bishop of Truro himself conducted the service. Two Members of Parliament attended, a minor duke and, of course, Lord Alfred and Sir Ralph Mountford. If Treskillen folk didn't wrest a meagre living from sea or land, they were employed on the Mountford estate and most fishermen were glad of a bit of part-time work when weather conditions made fishing impossible — all but George Trembarth! Emily remembered with pride her father's stubborn resistance.

'I'll not be exploited up at that house. We'll manage.' And they always had. 'We're as good as they are any day, and don't none of you forget it. If they'd pay decent wages now . . . '.

No use Sarah telling him she couldn't feed the family on his pride because he always provided a rabbit or pheasant for the pot, though it didn't do to enquire too closely where it came from. George's philosophy was simple enough — 'God gave this land to all of us. 'Tis only fate's quirk and accidental birth gave the Mountford's claim to it. They'll never miss a bit of what's ours by natural rights.'

Emily's eyes filled with tears as she stared at the names on the granite cross. How could the family carry on without their men?

11

'Life'll go on Emily. No choice.'

A comforting hand on her shoulder, a familiar voice.

'Harry! How did you guess what I was thinking?'

'It wasn't difficult. It's what we're all thinking.'

His dark eyes were bleak and sombre, looking past Emily out to sea.

'You and I, Emily, could both be out there. You'd sprained your ankle, I had to go to Truro for Dad. Why, Emily, why were we spared?'

'Perhaps as some small consolation to our families. I don't know Harry. I don't want to think about it.'

'You're right. It's the future that matters. My ma and gran, the little 'uns, your mother, Polly — you'll have to be the breadwinner now.'

'But how? The boat's gone. Dad's gone. The canning factory's not taking on any workers until the pilchards come in.'

'That'll be any day now — but you've no need to work at the cannery.

There's plenty of fish out there, and you're as good a fisherman as ever your brothers. You know this bay like your own face.'

'I told you — there's no boat. How can I fish without one and all the tackle? There's only the sculler, and that's no good.'

'What about insurance? Your dad should've kept that up to date.'

Emily looked doubtful. 'Dad wasn't a great one for making provision for the future. I don't know. Mother might. She hasn't said. It'll take time.'

'Then share my boat. I need a crew now Dad's gone. We'll be partners.'

'What'd folk say?'

'Hang what they'd say. You always went out in the boat with your dad, John and Matt.'

'That was different. They were my family.'

'Emmy, Emmy — please don't go to sea.'

Polly's frantic wail startled them. The young child had gathered enough

13

to know her precious only sister might go back to that angry sea — the sea that'd got her dad and John and Matthew. She clung to Emily's knees.

'You shan't, you shan't.'

'Polly, don't fret . . . nothing's decided. We're just talking . . . but we can't stop fishing, love. The sea's part of us Trembarths, in spite of what it's done. We'd best go, Harry. Aunt Maud!'

Over Polly's head, she pulled a wry face.

'She says she's got a plan for us. I wish they'd go back to Plymouth,' she said softly, for Harry's ears only.

'Not too keen on Auntie Maud?'

He fell into step beside her, a stocky figure who looked far more at home in his usual garb of fisherman's jersey and oilskins than in rough black Sunday-best serge suit and stiff celluloid collar.

'I don't really know her. She seems fond of Mother. She's a bit . . . '

Emily hesitated, not wanting to be disloyal. Maud was her aunt, and family. But Harry was her friend — far more important to her life and future than the aunt and uncle who'd suddenly materialised from far distant Devon!

'She's a bit too fond of telling us all what to do.'

'She'll have met her match in you then. It'll take a strong woman, or man for that matter, to boss you, Emily Trembarth!'

'Now then, that'll do.'

Emily smiled, sadness easing a little at the familiar banter. Life did have to go on — just so long as she could stay in Treskillen with her family and friends — friends like Harry. She looked up at him fondly.

'You'll be glad to get rid of that collar. It's making a red mark already.'

'I will, and I'll be glad to end this day, too.'

He jerked his head towards the granite monument.

'We'll never forget them, but they'd be the first to grant us our lives back, hard though it'll be to carry on without 'em.'

He stopped and turned to Emily, holding her back a little.

'Think hard about what I said — and the future. We have a future Emily, you and I. We . . . '

'I'll have to talk to Mother,' she interrupted swiftly, confused and alarmed by the serious and different quality of his look and tone.

For the first time ever, Emily felt uneasy with Harry.

'We'd better run on, or we'll be in bother with Aunt Maud.'

'I'll walk along with you. Shall I see you tomorrow? You'll be at the Huer's Stone to watch out for the pilchard shoals?'

'I promised Grandfather Trembarth I'd always take my turn around now. The shoals — they're overdue.'

'They'll come. Don't worry. I remember you as a tiny girl, standing on the cliff top waving your arms while your grandad waved his furze bush to show the fishermen which way the shoals moved. They were the days when the bay was awash with pilchards. The canneries couldn't keep up with 'em. We'd have starved without them. Our cellar used to be stocked out with pilchards — they'd last all through winter, salted down. Pity they aren't coming in like they used to do.'

'Harry, that's another worry, too — what if they never come back?'

'Don't be so gloomy. Trembarths always did bring them in in the end. It's a mystery to me how the fish come in year after year — all that way from the Atlantic, round the Scillies, to our bay.'

They had reached Emily's cottage. Aunt Maud stood ominously in the front doorway, arms folded, lips compressed.

'I told you not to be long, young lady. That cart'll be here directly to take us to the station. We've not much more than an hour or two.'

'I'm sorry, Aunt Maud, I thought you were staying over.'

'No chance of that, with the boarding house to run. I daren't think what'll be happening there with both of us away.'

'Mrs Broome.' Harry tipped his cap politely.

'I hope you weren't planning to be asked inside, young man. We've business to attend to — family business.'

'Aunt Maud!' Emily frowned at her aunt's rudeness.

Harry shook his head. 'I'll not be intruding . . . and I've my own family matters to attend to. I'll pay my respects to Mrs Trembarth another day. Emily, I'll be at the Huer's Stone tomorrow — midday.'

'I shall be there Harry — midday,' Emily called over her shoulder as she followed her aunt's broad disapproving back into the cottage.

2

The Trembarth's cottage stood granite solid in the centre of a row of six. Two stone steps led directly from street to door, and a tiny passageway of a hall ended in a fair-sized kitchen at the back.

Heat from the open range made the room suffocatingly hot, but Sarah Penrose hugged the fire's heat as though she'd never be warm again. Emily took her mother's icy hands and rubbed them between her own warm ones.

Will Broome, in shirt sleeves and waistcoat, forked slices of ham and potatoes in a giant cast iron frying pan on the oven range. The meat sizzled and spat, its fragrant pungency making Emily realise how hungry she was.

There'd been so much to see to since the accident, and so little money, they'd scarce had time or inclination to

19

cook or eat. They'd subsisted mainly on bread and cheese, and vegetables from the garden, although the women of the chapel had made hot soup daily for a week following the drownings.

'Smells good, Uncle Will.'

'There'll scarce be enough time to eat it,' her aunt grumbled, hacking a loaf into thick slices. 'You've been long enough chattering to your young man. You can make yourself useful now you're here. Kettle's boiled. Make the tea, and you, Polly, fetch the plates. Set them near your Uncle Will, then put out the knives and forks. There's no reason for idleness.'

Sarah rocked listlessly to and fro, her mind still numbed by the disaster. She was rudderless, simply waiting for someone else to take the reins.

Maud wasn't slow to take up the challenge. She'd been chafing in the wings ever since the funeral. Will had advised caution.

'See how things settle,' he'd said.

Well, that was nigh on a couple of

months ago, and as far as she could see, things had slid into chaos. Sarah and the girls seemed half starved, and Emily about to run wild. A firm hand was needed, and it'd be a relief to get them away from Cornwall!

'Right, now eat — all of it. You don't look as though you've had a proper meal since I don't know when.'

'Where's the money come from for all this?' Sarah asked dully.

'They tell me, in the village, Lord Mountford's promised money to all the families who've lost their men. You can pay me back then.'

'Dad wouldn't've liked to rely on Mountford charity,' Emily snapped.

'Shame on you Emily — such ingratitude. Lord Mountford at least knows his duty for once, and beggars can't be choosers, and you're as close to beggary as it's possible to be.'

'Maud,' Will remonstrated mildly. 'Emily's upset — they all are. It's been a bad day. Let's just enjoy the food now.'

For several minutes the only sounds were the clatter of cutlery and the steady tick of the grandfather clock in the corner. The chiming of the hour signalled the end of the peace.

Maud had been winding herself up during the pause. She carried on from where Will had stopped her.

'Point is, Will Broome, we can't afford to be as charitable as the likes of His Lordship,' she said with bitter disparagement, 'but it's family duty to help out. You should know, Emily, not only did your father leave you penniless, he left plenty of debts, too. In the village . . . '

'Won't there be insurance money? The boat was insured — Dad showed me the paper.'

'He may have shown you the policy, but he's not paid an instalment on it these last five years. There's naught to come from that. And there's two months' rent on this place, I hear. Lord Alfred Mountford's a humane man. He'll maybe not evict you right off, but he'll not be letting you stay rent free much longer.'

'Evict! You mean . . . we'll have to live somewhere else . . . ?'

'You silly girl. Of course you will. How did you think your mother'd manage? You're penniless. Paupers!'

'Maud . . . ' Will tried again, but she quelled him with a shake of her knife.

'No point soft-talking. It's nigh on six weeks since any money came into the house. It's time for straight thinking.'

Emily stared at her plate, all appetite vanished. Of course she knew there'd been no regular money coming in — even before the accident the fishing had been poor, but her mother hadn't said anything. She'd bought the necessities of life in the village — the garden had provided vegetables.

'Mother?' Emily appealed to the bowed black-clad figure.

Sarah, avoiding her daughter's eye, simply nodded.

'It's all true,' she said flatly.

'But we can pay off the debts with

Lord Mountford's money, then . . . '

'Then what?' her aunt asked.

'I'll work. I'll do anything.'

'That you will — but there's nothing for you here. Fishing's all you know, your ma says. Such nonsense — a girl going out in all weathers with a gang of men.'

Emily pushed back her chair and faced her aunt.

'There wasn't . . . isn't . . . anything wrong. The Treskillen fishermen accept me as one of them. I know you mean well, Aunt Maud, you and Uncle Will coming all the way from Plymouth for the funeral, and again for the service today, but we'll manage now.'

'How, I should be interested to hear?'

'I'm . . . I'm going to do it on a proper basis.'

'Do what, for heaven's sake?'

'I'm going to fish as a living. I can make a good one. Pilchards'll be in soon.'

Both aunt and uncle looked horrified.

'I'll work with Harry Rosevear, the lad you met at the gate. He'll let me use his boat till I have enough money for my own. We'll be partners. And mother can earn a bit — she's done sewing before.'

'Who can afford to pay for sewing in this village? You're talking nonsense girl. What a preposterous notion. A slip of a girl — a fisherman!'

'There's nothing wrong with me making a living at the fishing.'

'Well, we want you away from here, back to Devon where we Penroses belong.'

'You've no right . . . ' Emily's anger was rising like a storm tide.

Sarah knew her daughter and roused herself sufficiently to damp it down before it reached full flood.

'Emily, mind your manners. Listen to what Aunt Maud's got to say. And you should apologise.'

Her mother looked so wretchedly unhappy, guilt extinguished Emily's anger.

'I'm sorry, Aunt Maud. I didn't mean offence. I know you mean well.'

'You've had a sad day so we'll say no more about that. I warrant you're not your normal self. Now, I should think it's obvious to you by now that you can't stay here, so your Uncle Will and I have decided it'd be best if you were in Plymouth, with us at Broomehill — that's the name of our boarding house. The business does well, but an extra pair of hands'll be useful. Sarah will help out. Will needs a hand with cooking and waiting tables. Polly'll go to the school. There's plenty of fetching and carrying to be done in a boarding house — her legs are younger than mine.'

'Plymouth! I can't . . . ' Emily interrupted.

'Hear me out, miss. You're old enough to get a proper job. There's plenty of work in Plymouth, in one of the guest houses perhaps. I'll enquire around. A live-in job'd suit. We can only spare one room in the house for three of you.'

Emily, stunned with horror, heard all the advantages of a move to Plymouth — shops, more people, civilised town society, the protection of Maud and Will. Polly's eyes grew rounder and rounder, whether with wonder or dismay, it was hard to tell.

Maud poured herself more tea, without pausing for breath.

'So, you'll agree it'd be best for everyone. A week or so to clear up here, settle what debts you can, drop us a line to tell us your train time, and Will'll meet you at the station. Now we must be moving, else we'll miss our train.'

Emily, calmly, though her heart thumped madly, said, 'Aunt Maud, we can't come to Plymouth. Our home's here in Treskillen. It's very kind . . .'

'You'll do as you're bid. You've no say in it. It's decided. Tell her, Sarah. Seems she don't believe me.'

'Mother!' Emily rushed over to her. 'Please don't make us leave here. I couldn't bear it.'

'I'm sorry Emily, but Maud's right. I don't want to stay here. I hate the place.'

'Mother! Hate Treskillen?'

'I've never liked it. Oh, it was all right when your father was here, and the boys. We were a proper family then. What are we now? Three poor females. That's what Treskillen's done! How long do you think we could manage here on our own?'

'We could, we could! Please — just a few more weeks, then, if we really can't manage, we'll go to Plymouth. Mother, please.'

'No! The longer we stay, the more debt will crush us.'

'But there's the fishing with Harry. There's still money to be made.'

Sarah, more animated, put her hands on the young girl's shoulders.

'Do you want to kill me, too? You'd have to go out in all weathers. Don't you think I've had enough of lying awake listening to the rising winds at night, watching the skies threaten by day? How do you think I'd feel if I let you go to sea? Bad enough when your dad and brothers were with you. I've suffered over a quarter of a century of it. No more, Emily, no more.'

She buried her head in her hands, and Emily knew that the wonderful notion of partnering Harry in a fishing venture had been no more than a silly, foolish dream. Of course, it was impossible!

'You're right. I see it was thoughtless — but I could get a job here, at the canneries. Don't decide yet . . . stay a while longer.'

'Canneries aren't taking on any more labour. Even I know that, and I don't live here,' Maud interjected. 'You need money now. And there's the cart come for us. Look sharp, Will.'

Maud pulled on her coat, settled her black summer straw at a daunting angle, and pulled on dark cotton gloves. She bent to kiss her sister.

'We'll expect you in a week then. Any bother — drop a line to Broomehill, not that there will be. Polly, you be a good girl. Mind your ma. And Emily, I shall have a job ready for you as soon as you arrive.'

Emily suffered a perfunctory embrace and followed her aunt to the front door, and waved as the horse plodded down the lane towards the village.

'See you next week,' she called.

'Not me, you won't,' she said to herself, but the prospect of what was to happen to the three of them was weighing heavily on her.

★ ★ ★

'So you see why it's not possible, Harry. I couldn't do it to Mother — not so soon.'

'It's a shame. I've got my eye on a bigger boat. We could sail out farther, where the herring are. The insurance agent says there'll be a tidy sum . . . '

'Your dad was more prudent than mine. I think you should go ahead. Jonathan'll be able to help you in a year or so.'

'Thank God he was too young to have gone out that day. I tell Ma we must count our blessings — she's two men left.'

Emily nodded, but never took her eyes off the blue waters beyond the beaches and harbour. She was on duty as the look-out, watching for the dark shadows on the sea which heralded the coming of the pilchards.

The beach directly below the Huer's Stone was the usual place the pilchards came to, and men and women were already stationed by their boats, waiting to shoot the seine nets to trap the precious shoals.

'I'm sure today's the day. I just feel it. Now the memorial service is over, we have to start afresh. Pilchards coming in'll mean we've paid our dues to the sea — for a while at least. You should be down on the beach, too, Harry.'

'Young Jon's standing by the boat for me. See him, down there. I can be with him in a couple of minutes — if and when the shoal comes in.'

'It will — I know it.'

Emily climbed up half a dozen rough-hewn steps to a flat stone platform. Shielding her eyes against the sun's glare, she picked up the traditional furze bush, ready to use it as a pointer to the shoals, so the fishermen on the beach would know where to shoot their nets. For a while she concentrated on sweeping the horizon. Her grandad had taught her exactly what to look for.

'Nothing yet.'

She squatted down on the sun-warmed granite, her gaze never leaving the blue water. Harry joined her, and she leaned companionably against him. She'd already told him of Aunt Maud's plan. It'd been good to confide.

'I hate the idea. I'll not go to

Plymouth. I've got to think of something else. A live-in job as a boarding house skivvy — horrible! I'd never see Polly or Mother or Treskillen . . . '

'You shan't go to Plymouth. Why it's the other side of the country. I'd never see you again.'

He looked down at her downcast face, so pretty now. She'd grown up a lot since her dad and brothers had died. If she went away she'd be lost to him, he was sure of that. He put a protective arm around her shoulder.

'If you've got to leave the cottage, why not try for a job up at the Hall? My cousin Hetty's a parlour maid. She's leaving soon, emigrating to America with her man.'

She pulled a face.

'Mountford Hall! Dad wouldn't've approved of me working for them.'

'Hetty says it's not so bad. Food's good and they have a bit of fun. It'd be one way of staying close by. If you didn't like it you wouldn't have to stay.'

With an abrupt movement she got up and stood on tip-toe.

'Look, by Gribben's Rock . . . there's ripples . . . see . . . surface movement. Ah, I'm not sure. It's gone smooth again! They must come in on this tide. I'm so certain. Grandad used to say he could smell them.'

Harry stood uncertainly, watching her, not the ocean. He said slowly, 'There is another way you can stay here in Treskillen . . . '

'What's that? Look, the ripples . . . darker patches of sea . . . I'm almost sure it's the pilchards. In a minute . . . '

'You could marry me.'

There was silence. The bush in Emily's hand dropped. She felt Harry's hands on her shoulders turn her to face him.

'I always thought . . . one day . . . right back when we were little, playing weddings in that cave. Remember, you always called it our sea chapel. Emily, we were both spared the drownings — saved for something. It's our destiny. I know it's soon, but you can't leave me now.'

A tremendous cacophony of honking and shouting made him spin round.

'What the devil?'

Emily, caught off balance, stumbled against him, clutching his arm in stupefied amazement, eyes round as dinner plates. She stared and stared, pilchards and proposal both driven out of her head by an astonishing sight.

'Harry, it's . . . it's a motor car . . . two of them!' Her voice rose to a squeak as she held on to Harry like grim death. 'I've never seen one before. What a racket. What are they doing up here?'

'Must be people from the Hall. Stupid idiots. The cliffs are no place for those stupid contraptions. I know Sir Ralph's got one, though I've not seen it. What are the blithering fools doing?'

Two open cars bumped along the rough track towards the stone. Some considerable way behind was a solitary horseman, but both Harry's and Emily's attention was riveted on the chugging, noisy horseless carriages.

'They're racing each other. One of 'em'll be over the cliff afore long. They're too near the edge. Haven't they got any brains?' Harry waved his arms. 'Get over, get back — slow down. They'll smash into the stone and scare the shoals away with that racket. Get down Emily.'

'I can't. Stop them, Harry. Make them stop. See — the pilchards, they're here at last.'

Turning away from the oncoming motor cars she waved her furze bush and shouted down to the beach

'Hevva, hevva . . . the shoals . . . the pilchards are in. Coming straight on from Gribben's Rock. Quick — hevva, hevva.'

Here words were drowned by squealing breaks, slamming doors, shouts and screams.

'We won, we won. We beat you to the stone.'

'No, you cheated.'

Emily swung round.

'Be quiet,' she cried, the shock of the amazing new invention fading to insignificance before the joy of the shoals. 'They can't hear me.'

A crowd of young people, dressed in a height of fashion never before seen at the Huer's Stone, tumbled on to the grass.

A cry went up below, boats were pushed into the water, and the seine nets shot in the direction pointed out by the furze bush. Now the fishermen had to haul the leaping writhing mass to the surface and heave them into boats. The shoal was so big, many more fish were driven up to the beach where women and children had buckets a-plenty to catch the surplus.

Emily fairly danced with excitement.

'Harry, get down there. Look, Jonathan's waiting. He can't launch the boat by himself.'

'You haven't answered me.'

The party from the two vehicles

pressed close, one or two scrambling up on to the stone platform for a better view of the beach. Others leaned dangerously close to the cliff, each peering at the frantic activity below.

A girl on the stone jostled Emily. 'Ugh. Those slimy fish. How horrid.'

'Phew!' A young man affectedly held his nose. 'What a stink — even up here. It'll spoil the picnic.'

'Please — get off the rock. I need to make sure the shoal's still coming in the right direction.'

Emily was suddenly conscious of her shabby skirt and heavy clogs against the girl's fashionable summer frock and white sandals.

'Don't you dare talk to me like that.' The girl glared at her. 'We're staying at Lord Mountford's.'

'I don't care where you're staying. You're in the way here.'

'What cheek. Herbert, tell this impudent girl who you are.'

'I should do as the young lady asks. She has a job to finish.'

It was a deeper, more mature voice, with a touch of familiar West Country burr, unlike the strange accents of the others. The horse-rider looked severely at the fashion-clad girl, then touched his riding hat to Emily.

'I see the pilchards have arrived at last. Cecily, do get down from there. I thought you were all heading for a picnic.'

'We were,' the girl pouted, but obediently did as she was told. 'On that beach, but it's covered in smelly fish.'

The rider leaned down to her. 'That smelly fish is life and death to Treskillen. Pilchards might not be on the menu at your daddy's smart London house, but it's these folks' livelihood, Miss Westerridge. So I should take your hampers farther along the track. I'll join you later, when you've shifted those confounded noisy vehicles out of the way.'

The man sat easily on his large chestnut roan, a commanding figure, a little older than the other members of the motor party, Emily guessed. Dark eyes smiled at her.

'Sorry you were disturbed. I'm glad to see it'll be a big catch. Treskillen deserves some luck.' He glanced at Harry's fisher garb. 'Won't you be missing out?'

Emily came back to reality. She'd forgotten Harry was still there! She gave him a little push.

'Quick — I'm counting on you for our pilchards, too.'

'Don't worry, we'll share the catch — and remember, I want an answer.'

Emily blushed, aware the horseman was watching. In a swift movement Harry took Emily in his arms and kissed her on the lips, then was off, sprinting down the cliff path to the beach, and was there in seconds.

'Your young man's done that a time or two,' the rider commented admiringly. 'Cliff path I mean — of course!'

'He's not my . . . '

But the man reined his horse in

tightly, offered his hand.

'I'm Noah Templeton, staying at Mountford Hall.'

Emily hesitated. It was common local knowledge Sir Ralph Mountford and his young wife entertained a lot. Lady Constance Mountford's father was Lord Mayor of London, and her social circle was wide, though Emily had never before been in such close contact with anyone from the Hall.

Relations between Treskillen villagers and Mountford gentry and their friends were strictly limited to employment. Although Emily's cottage was a mere dozen or so miles from Mountford Hall, socially they might have inhabited different planets. But this man was friendly and open, with no sign of stand-offishness. She put her hand in his, and he shook it solemnly.

'From Exeter,' he volunteered. 'Not part of that giddy lot.'

'Er . . . Emily Trembarth.'

'Well, Miss Trembarth, I hope we'll

41

meet again. Well done at the Huer today.'

He skilfully manoeuvred his horse away from the stone and, with a final wave, cantered off in the same direction taken by the motor cars.

Emily watched his broad back rising rhythmically with the muscled movement of the beautiful roan. She felt a pang of envy. On such a sunfilled day, to picnic, carefree among the rocks, swim, laze in the sun — and there'd be lovely food in those hampers, even champagne maybe!

She shrugged her shoulders and set off down the cliff. At least there'd be fresh pilchards for tea that night. She'd dig up new potatoes from Matt's great joy, his vegetable garden. At least they wouldn't go hungry this week. Beyond the one week, she didn't dare think. Harry's proposal she filed away at the back of her mind — to consider later.

It'd be a busy enough day getting the pilchards up to the salting sheds on the harbour, preserving the fish in barrels for the long winter months. Would she still be in Treskillen in the winter? Even though her future was so uncertain, Emily's step was lighter than it had been for weeks as she ran down the path to join Treskillen villagers on the beach.

3

Only a week's grace — a mere seven days before Aunt Maud's deadline for the Trembarth emigration to Plymouth. Emily had hoped that after the memorial service her mother would slide back into Treskillen routine, and decide to stay, but Sarah Trembarth had made up her mind.

The day after Maud left she began clearing the cottage, selling her belongings to settle her husband's debts. It saddened Emily to see all the familiar things trundled away in barrows to grace other people's cottages.

One night, when young Polly was tucked up in bed, Sarah tried to explain how she felt to her elder daughter.

'We must accept the changes in our lives as God's will, Emily, and look to the future. Mine and Polly's is with

Maud. I've told you how she cared for me and my sisters and brothers when our mother died. I was the youngest of ten and only a year old when Maud had to pick up the reins. She held the family together, and wouldn't marry Will Broome until I'd married and most of your uncles had emigrated. She was too old then to have children of her own. She wants me with her and I'm pulled back to her now, but I've realised I've been selfish expecting you to come, too. You don't have to if you're so set against it.'

Emily, scouring out an empty cupboard, jerked her head round in surprise. 'Not come to Plymouth with you?'

'Not against your will. You're seventeen, old enough to make your own way. Susan Rosevear tells me there's a job at Mountford Hall. I've no objection to you trying to get work there. Maud'll be upset — she's as set against Mountford Hall as your dad was, but if I explain about you and Harry . . . well, 'tis natural you want to be near him.'

'There's naught between us . . . no understanding.'

'There doesn't need to be. I've got eyes, even though they've been so tear-squalled lately. I can see the way he looks at you.'

'I can't marry just to stay here.'

'But isn't that what you want more than anything — to stay in Treskillen?'

'I . . . I don't know.'

What did she want? She did love Treskillen and Cornwall, but lately she'd wondered — a restlessness had invaded her soul. She remembered the bright young people at the Huer's Stone that day — the man on horseback. What sort of lives did they have? Would she ever find that out at Mountford Hall — in service?

But the alternative was Plymouth — in service, in a boarding house. Either way it was the break-up of her family — and there wasn't room for her at Aunt Maud's. Impulsively, she decided, 'I'll beg a ride on the mail cart to Mountford Hall tomorrow — if you're sure.'

'I'm sure. Polly and I'll manage very well with Maud, and you can always visit — or change your mind if you're not happy at the Hall.'

★ ★ ★

It was a wonderful dream. Dark silver pilchards in a navy-blue sea, swarming into Treskillen harbour. She was hauling nets with her father and Matt. They were laughing. An azure sky, hot sun on her back — then someone shaking her . . .

'Emily, wake up. It's five o'clock . . . the week-end party . . . so much to do.'

The dream vanished into the sunlight air of her imagination — and she remembered. Clarrie was shaking her. Clarrie was a housemaid, too, at Mountford Hall, and she and Emily had been there two months.

'I'll go start the fires. Don't be long,' Clarrie said.

Emily yawned hugely, but swung her feet on to the bare boards of the attic room she shared with Clarrie.

In her first days at Mountford Hall she had been homesick for Treskillen, her mother, and Polly, but taking each day as it came, she'd gradually settled in, and with the camaraderie of her fellow servants, had even begun to feel at home. And Harry's cousin had been right — the food was lovely!

A pang of guilt pricked her as she tip-toed down the back stairs to the kitchen. Harry was due at the Hall today to deliver his catch of crab and lobsters ordered for the week-end house party guests from London. He'd be bound to see her, and be bound to ask his habitual question.

There was a great deal of frivolity at the staff eight o'clock breakfast. London visitors and their accompanying servants always caused excitement. Chauffeurs, valets, and ladies' maids brought more than a whiff of cosmopolitan sophistication to the remote corner of Cornwall. Courtships often blossomed, and the young folk lived in the hope of romance.

'D'you think the ghosts'll come this time? Often 'appens when there be guests.' Martha, that lowest of the low in the downstairs hierarchy, a tweeny, looked apprehensive.

'Don't talk silly. There are no ghosts,' Mrs Miller, the housekeeper, scolded.

'There's Ermentrude and her poor babby.'

'That'll do, Martha. There's no time for that sort of talk — and you'll get the sack if Lord Alfred hears you. So go on about your business, all of you. There's plenty to do before the guests arrive tomorrow. Emily, you may take in the fish from your young man, but no lingering mind.'

Reliable as ever, Harry turned up on the dot of twelve with a laden cart.

'Some fuss out there,' he grumbled

as he hoisted the baskets on to his shoulders.

'We're topsy-turvey for the London party. How's your mother?'

'Grieving, but managing. Your folk in Plymouth doing all right?'

'Settling. Mother says she's better away from Treskillen — no memories to remind her. Aunt Maud's disowned me because I'm working at Mountford Hall. I don't know why.'

'You shouldn't be on bad terms with your family. I'll take you to visit on your day off. You should make it up with your aunt.'

'I haven't done anything — and I only get half a day. P'raps later.'

'You should set the day for us to wed. It'd be the answer to everything. Our cottage is roomy enough. Ma likes you — you'd be company for her.'

He put his arm round her.

'Not here.'

Emily pulled away. What had happened to the idea of the business partnership? Sharing the fishing?

'Emily!' Clarrie rushed over. 'Mrs Miller wants you on duty in the dining room. I'm to fetch cream from the dairy, to serve lunch. You'll need to change to your upstairs uniform.'

'Upstairs uniform! Sounds like a danged prison,' Harry exclaimed.

' 'Tis a bit, but I'm not serving a life sentence.'

'I'll come up for you a week Sunday.'

But Emily was already running towards the house . . .

She stood unobtrusively by the sideboard, demure in black dress and starched cap, waiting for the butler, Mr Williams, to nod his commands. This was one of the bonuses of working at Mountford Hall, peeking into the lives of the gentry.

Three people were seated in splendid state at one end of the long dining table. Lord Alfred Mountford, head of the household, ate little. He was in a wheel-chair today, and Emily thought he looked old and ill. Sir Ralph, his

51

son, waded steadily through a four-course luncheon, quite impervious to the nagging of his beautiful, young wife, Lady Constance. The daughter of the Lord Mayor of London was used to society on a grand scale. She kept up a barrage of requests and demands for her friends throughout the meal.

Suddenly, old Lord Alfred threw down his napkin.

'Coffee in the library, Williams, please. No, no need to ring the bell. The girl can push this thing along to the library. What's your name?'

He shot a fierce glance at Emily.

'Emily Trembarth, sir.'

'Trembarth? Ah, yes. On the roll of honour on the monument. Father and brothers, too?'

Emily nodded.

'Well, come along. You'll get the hang of the chair.' He nodded to his son and daughter-in-law. 'If you'll excuse me. I'm sure you can get along with your social plans without me.'

Emily had just about mastered the

layout of Mountford Hall, and never ceased to marvel at the spacious grandeur of it all. Efficiently, she propelled the chair along the carpeted corridors towards the library. Lord Alfred pushed the double doors aside impatiently.

'The fire, Emily, by the fire. Can't seem to get warm today.'

'Shall I put more coals on, sir?'

'If you'd be so good.'

She cast covert glances around the room with its deep, recessed shelves crammed with leather-bound volumes, deep armchairs, magnificent desk in the wide window.

'D'you like what you see, Emily Trembarth?'

'I'm sorry, sir. I . . .'

'I see you admire my library. Shows your taste. Never been in here?'

'To dust, sir. I . . . I do like the room. Very much.'

'I've not seen you before. How long've you been here?'

He was leaning forward. The fire

gave his face a healthier glow — a strong face still in spite of his years, but stern and sad somehow. Emily wondered how anyone could be sad in all this magnificence, with so many people to satisfy every whim.

'Two months, sir.'

'I'm sorry about your kin. How old are you, child?'

'Eighteen.'

'You're a child to me, Emily.'

He was silent so long staring at the flames, Emily bobbed a curtsey and turned to go, but he put a hand out.

'Wait a moment. I . . . '

The butler came in and frowned at Emily.

'Coffee, my lord?' Aside to Emily, severely, 'Downstairs, please.'

'I kept her here, Williams.'

The old man seemed about to say more, but after one more keen look at Emily, turned back to the fire, holding out veined hands to the blaze.

With a final bob she left the room, deciding she liked Lord Alfred

Mountford. What a pleasure it would be to sit in that fine room with him and talk about his life! She knew from downstairs gossip that he'd spent much of his life in far-off places, but there was no time for dreaming that day!

She was back below stairs with not a moment's peace until well after midnight when finally all was set for the London invasion. Some of the servants lingered.

Martha still had the unquiet spirits of the past on her mind and made mugs of cocoa, anxious to keep everyone downstairs.

'There's no such things as ghosts,' Jacob kindly reassured her, 'but there's legends galore here, and the London folk like that.'

'What sort of legends?'

Emily was curious.

'Mostly from the Civil War — cavaliers hiding from Cromwell's men. 'Twas reckoned that the bones of a man and woman were found in an old priest hole under the conservatory out yonder. Supposedly a young Mountford daughter perished with her lover, rather than risk seeing him die at Puritan hands. Folk who've had too much cheese for supper do say they've glimpsed a young couple in costume of the day.'

'How dreadful!' Clarrie bit her lip.

'No.' Jacob was enjoying his captive audience. ' 'Tis said they're happy spirits — united, forever young.'

'Tell them about Ermentrude.' Martha was round-eyed.

The footman hesitated. 'That's more nonsense.'

'Tell them. Visitors to the Hall swear they've seen her, and her babby.'

'It's an old tale. Lord Mountford don't like to hear tell of it. Years ago, or not so long ago, no-one knows exactly when. A young serving girl was well . . . taken . . . by a Mountford. There was a baby, and the girl was turned out of the village. Mountford disowned her, as did her own kin. She threw herself and the infant down the well in the yard, by the dairy. That's all, and it's time we were in our beds. Look sharp now.'

Jacob had heard Mr Williams' step outside. The butler strongly disapproved of downstairs gossip — especially when it touched badly on his revered noble family.

But Martha managed to whisper to Emily, 'And the poor ghost of Ermentrude . . . that's not her real name neither . . . comes here with her little wet babby . . . looking for vengeance. That's why she comes when there's visitors — to bring shame on the Mountfords.'

Emily's sense of justice was roused by the tale. The powerful Mountfords against a poor servant girl! The tale had probably been much embroidered down the years, but there seemed no doubt of its truth.

Next evening, Emily caught the excitement of a very different world as she moved discreetly round the vast reception hall with a tray of sherry wine. She'd never seen nor imagined such rich elegance! The ball, attended by all the local county notables, was the highlight of the visitors' week-end.

Emily had never seen Lady Constance so animated and sparkling. Even Sir Ralph, usually so sober and silent, smiled on his guests. Lord Alfred, aristocratic in white tie and tails, leaned heavily on his cane, but seemed happy to be surrounded by old friends.

Emily tried to concentrate on her work, but the scene was so brilliantly scintillating, she found it hard not to be distracted. There was a single glass left on her tray when a dark sleeve with white starched cuff and gold cufflinks reached for it.

'Well, well, Miss Trembarth, from the Huer's Stone.'

A familiar West Country voice, warm and friendly. To the majority of the guests the tray-bearer was invisible! But the horse-rider from the day of the shoals came and smiled directly at her — Noah Templeton — the name came easily into her head. Across the room, the butler frowned at her.

'I . . . yes . . . I must go . . . er, Mr Templeton. I . . . I have to refill the tray.'

He said easily, 'Are you working here — just for this evening's dance?'

'I . . . work here . . . permanently.'

His brows lifted fractionally, but he stood aside to let her pass.

The next time Emily saw Noah Templeton was in the ballroom, dancing with a pretty auburn-haired girl whom she recognised as the haughty girl called Cicely, who'd climbed up on to the stone and expressed her disdain of the slimey pilchards. She was laughing up at Noah as they twirled together.

Emily's legs and feet ached with running up and down stairs with trays and glasses, and plates of savouries for the late supper-spread in the dining room — but she knew she longed to be part of that dancing throng, longed, for the first time in her life, to wear a long, silk gown with a nipped-in waist and cascading skirt, and have her hair cunningly pinned up with flowers. It was a strange sensation for the wild tomboy of Treskillen to feel envy for those rich and pampered women, and Emily didn't particularly like the feeling. She wished the dance was over, and they could all go to bed.

'Bottle of champagne called for in the conservatory, Emily.'

Mr Williams snapped his fingers and passed her a silver salver with crystal glasses and napkin covered bottle.

'Fast as you can now, and then Mrs Miller wants a hand in the kitchen.'

There was no-one in the conservatory when she got there. The supper gong had sounded a few minutes earlier, and most people would be in the dining-room. A figure stepped out of the shadows — Noah Templeton.

'Miss Emily — again. With champagne, too.'

'Ordered for you, sir?'

'No, but I'll take the opportunity — as there's no-one else here. I wouldn't like you to carry it all the way back again.'

As he tore off the foil and untwisted the wire at the top, Emily gave a hardly perceptible bob and turned away.

'Just a second. Why don't you join me? There are two glasses. You look as though you've been working hard enough all night. Here . . .'

He poured out the golden bubbly wine and held out a stemmed glass.

Emily eyed it — and him — with suspicion. What was he playing at? Did he want to get her the sack?

'Thank you, sir, but Sir Ralph, Lady Constance . . . wouldn't be at all pleased.'

'Why not? They aren't here anyway.'

'You're a guest. I . . . I'm a . . .'

'Servant? No rights at all? I'm disappointed in you, Emily. By the Huer's Stone you struck me as an independent girl. I'm a guest, as you say, and I'm offering you a sip of wine because you'd like it. Nothing wrong in that.'

61

Emily was confused. Personally, she didn't see anything wrong either, but she also knew this sort of mingling with the guests would be severely frowned on by both upstairs and downstairs hierarchy.

'It's kind of you — sir, but I have to be getting on.'

'Emily!' Lady Constance's voice was frigid enough to turn the champagne to ice. 'What are you doing in here?'

'Mr Williams sent me with the champagne.'

'That was some time ago. I saw you leave the ballroom. It is not your place to linger and annoy my guests. Get back immediately.'

'Constance!' Noah exploded crossly. 'She is not annoying me. I asked Emily to stay.'

'Whatever for? Really, your radical ideas will get you into trouble one day. If you must harbour such politically outrageous, nonsensical notions, please keep them confined to your own household. Don't attempt to implement

62

them here at Mountford Hall.'

'For goodness' sake, this is the twentieth century. You'll have to change with the times. Constance . . . '

'Never!'

Her Ladyship's face was cold with anger. Emily stood, her own fury seething up in her as Lady Constance's hard, angry stare bored into her.

'Don't you just stand there, girl. Go back downstairs at once.'

'Look, Constance . . . '

There was rage in Noah's voice, but Emily wasn't waiting any longer. As she turned to go, it was Constance's voice which rang out over Noah's.

'I hope your wife, Noah, knows how to treat the servant class, otherwise I cannot vouch for your future domestic comforts.'

Emily's fists clenched with tension.

'I'll not stay,' she muttered to herself as she swung the door forward. 'I'll not stay here another day!'

4

Emily's anger kept her from the sleep her tired body demanded. She couldn't forget the contemptuous words spoken by Lady Constance, and in particular — 'Noah's wife'!

George Trembarth had instilled into his daughter a sense of her own worth — 'as good as the next, and don't ever forget it', and he'd told her that though servants and masters there were always bound to be, mutual respect and equality under God's eyes should be the cement of the bond between them. There'd been no respect in Lady Constance's tone and frigid look as she'd put Emily firmly in her place below stairs that night.

Emily, since working at Mountford Hall, was aware of a creeping discontent. She could leave and marry — set up her own home, but it'd be Harry's, and his mother's. Did she want that? When Lady Constance's words crashed into her brain she'd thought she did, anything to be out of the present situation, but in honesty, she wasn't so sure.

At Mountford Hall she'd seen such different ways of life — the visitors from London, Noah Templeton, even Harry's cousin whose job she'd taken, had escaped to America. Think of that — life in America — another continent! She'd read that in America everyone was equal, with equal opportunity to make his or her way in life. Could such a dream be true? Would Harry ever leave Treskillen?

It was only weeks earlier that her own aim had been never to leave the village. Why wasn't that enough now? It was no good, sleep had totally eluded her and it was practically dawn. She might as well get up. There'd be plenty to do downstairs — all the breakfasts to see to.

Cautiously, she eased out of bed. No

point in waking Clarrie from her happy dreams of the life she would have with her beloved Jacob!

Dawn was lighting up the sky when she slipped out of the back door of the servants' quarters. The morning air smelled delicious and Emily was sorely tempted to leave there and then. It would be perfect at Huer's Rock and Harry would be pleased to see her.

She quickened her step. She was nearly at the gate. Don't look back. They'll never miss you, there are so many other servants. But there were lots of guests, extra work for Clarrie and Mrs Miller, and Martha, and the rest. Was it fair to leave them in the lurch? She knew in her heart she couldn't just walk out — after all, Lord Alfred had been kind, and Sir Ralph wasn't a bad sort. She mustn't let Lady Constance get her down.

Emily turned to look back at the Hall. In the dawn's lustrous pink it looked benign and graceful, mullioned windows already winking in the early sun. It was as though the Hall was pulling her back.

Then she saw it, gasped, cried out, started to run as fast as she possibly could.

'Help!' she cried out, arms flailing as she flew up the path.

Someone had to be awake at the Hall! She was still a long way off from the back door . . . she tried to call out again but her breath was strained. Doubled up with a painful stitch, she burst into the deserted servants' hall, through the green baize door into the main hall. Picking up the gong, she banged as hard as she could.

'Fire! Fire!' she yelled out over the booming sound. 'Help! Quickly!'

She could smell smoke now. She'd seen it first at Lord Alfred's window.

At last, Mr Williams emerged from his room, blinking, tousled, so different from his immaculate daytime self.

'Emily! What . . . ?'

'Fire . . . quick . . . upstairs . . . Lord Alfred's room!'

67

She turned and ran, taking the main stairs in great bounds. She banged on all the doors, heard the gong booming below, and Mr Williams rousting out his staff. She ran towards Lord Alfred's room and pushed open the door. The heat leaped out at her, scorching her face, forcing her to step back. Flames were at the window, burning fabric dropping on the bed, where Lord Alfred lay half in, half out.

Shielding her face, she ran to the bed. He was unconscious. Smoke made her heave and choke.

'Here,' she called out. 'Quickly, oh!'

The breeze from the open window fanned the flames, blew the burning drapes towards the bed. Bracing herself, she flung off the smouldering top covers, yanked the under sheet and pulled it hard, kneeling to take the impact of the body before it hit the floor. Quickly she wrapped the other side of the sheet around Lord Alfred and pulled him unceremoniously towards the door.

Then there were willing hands to help. She stepped back, saw Noah's grim face just before she was smothered by a thick blanket. Hands beat her body and head. She couldn't breathe. She felt herself lifted bodily, carried jerkily, along, down, and out into the blessed smoke-free air.

Gently, she was set on her feet and the blanket was removed. She saw Noah's eyes, anxious, his hands on her hair.

'Emily . . . I thought for a minute . . . but it's not too bad . . . just singed a bit. But your hands, they're burned. Stay here. I must go back. There's a doctor in the house party and the fire engines should be here soon. Are you all right?'

She nodded. 'His Lordship?'

'I don't know, but he'd surely be dead but for you. You're a brave girl, Emily Trembarth. There are pumps in the outhouses . . . water in the well.'

He sprinted off, bumping into people streaming out of the hall in their nightclothes, a few in dressing gowns. Sir Ralph and Mr Williams directed a bucket chain, but to Emily, their efforts appeared puny against the flames. She saw Clarrie, who rushed over to her.

'Emily, thank God! You weren't in bed. I didn't know . . . oh . . . your poor hands!'

'They're all right, truly. The fire must have started in his Lordship's room. I saw the smoke from the garden. I couldn't get anyone to hear. I shouted and shouted.'

'Dead as logs from last night, I daresay. Emily, there's no water in the well. Jacob tried to pump it up. It's bone dry.'

'But all that rain last week. How can it be dry?'

'Ermentrude's curse, no doubt, Martha'll say. Perhaps 'twas she started the fire, too.'

'Clarrie! More like Lord Alfred smoking his cigars in bed.'

Shrilling bells heralded the fire cart and, as the sun rose into full daylight, order began to return to the chaotic scene.

Once water was pumping up from the lake, the firemen brought the blaze swiftly under control. Lord Alfred was treated by the local doctor, then taken to the cottage hospital for observation and rest. Under Mr Williams' firm guidance, any panic amongst the staff was dealt with by issuing long lists of clear-up tasks to be done as fast as possible and food, the general panacea, was prepared in the form of a mammoth Sunday breakfast.

Emily's hands were attended to in the library, by the Mountford family's own physician, who was staying as one of the guests at the Hall's weekend party. Still grime-streaked from smoke and soot, Sir Ralph nevertheless stayed whilst the doctor applied salve and bandages to Emily's fingers.

'You were instrumental in saving my father's life, Emily. We are very grateful for your prompt action in going straight to his room. His Lordship asked after you especially before he was taken to the hospital.'

'Thank you, Sir. I hope he'll be all right.'

'I've telephoned the cottage hospital. They're quite satisfied with his condition. He's suffering from shock, and there's a slight breathing problem caused by the smoke. Miraculously — no burns. I shall instruct Mr Williams to give you light duties until your hands are quite better.'

'Thank you, Sir.'

Emily had hardly noticed her blistered palms. They stung now, and she was thankful it had been no worse. But in this condition, she'd have to stay at the Hall for a while. Escape to Treskillen was out of the question.

Lady Constance came into the study and frowned when she saw Emily.

'What is that girl doing in here? I've sent Dr Moss down to the servants' quarters to see if anyone is hurt. This girl always seems to be in the wrong place . . .'

'Constance! It was Emily who pulled Father out of his blazing room, just in time! There was no-one else about. We should be grateful.'

'And what was she doing on the upstairs corridor in the middle of the night?' Constance asked sharply.

'I'd been out in the garden early. I couldn't sleep. I was coming back to the house and I saw smoke coming from Lord Alfred's room. I tried to rouse the household but everyone must have been sound asleep. I'm sure you wouldn't have wished me to leave his Lordship . . .'

'Of course not,' Sir Ralph interrupted quickly. 'Constance, I'm sure our guests will be needing you. I shall see that Emily returns downstairs as soon as Sir Robert here has finished.'

Lady Constance's rigid back and door-slamming exit made it perfectly clear what she thought of the situation, and Emily wondered if, in fact, she would have any choice about leaving her job at Mountford Hall. From her

Ladyship's hostile looks, dismissal was in the offing.

Seconds after Lady Constance had left, Noah Templeton entered. He was even more begrimed than Sir Ralph, and his open shirt was torn at the shoulder, but he smiled, and Emily smiled back. Noah never made her feel inferior, as Lady Constance did.

'Ah! The heroine of the hour. I hope you are duly grateful to Miss Trembarth, Ralph. I dread to think, but for her, what . . . '

'Indeed, yes, and I'm sure Father will want to thank her himself as soon as he's home.'

'Please, sir, I should be getting back.'

Emily was suddenly conscious of her unkempt hair and dirty face — and she was feeling hungry, too. Mrs Miller's lovely scrambled eggs and kedgeree was all at once much more to her taste than Sir Ralph's thanks.

'I don't suppose Emily's had time for breakfast.' Noah looked at her shrewdly. 'I don't know how your housekeeper's managed it, Ralph, but there's splendid Sunday breakfast in spite of everything.'

'Of course. Off you go now, Emily, and don't forget, his Lordship will be sure to want to thank you personally when he comes home.'

Emily went back to the kitchen, and the three men went in search of their belated Sunday breakfast.

A week later it was as though the fire had never been, although when Lord Alfred came home from hospital a new suite of rooms had to be prepared for him. Workmen were already busy restoring and repairing fire damage, but outwardly Mountford Hall was its serene and noble self, the only evidence of the disaster, blackened stone and some blank windows at the rear.

Lord Alfred's new rooms now over-looked the front of the house, and it was there Emily was summoned the day after he returned to the Hall. She was sorry to see Lady Constance sitting in an armchair by the bed as she made her bob to the old man, who was propped up on pillows in bed.

'Emily Trembarth, my dear girl. Come right over here. Constance, you've no need to stay now. I want to talk to Emily.'

'Of course I must stay. Don't be so foolish. You mustn't keep the girl long. She has work to do, and you shouldn't be overtired.'

'Constance, I don't think . . . '

He stopped and shrugged. He did still feel very weak and he could ill afford to lose what strength remained. There was something important he had to do.

'Emily, I have to thank you for saving my life — but for you I'd have been a heap of cinders.'

'Father-in-law, I'm sure we shouldn't have let . . . '

'Tush! You were all dead to the world.'

'If you hadn't been smoking a cigar before you went to sleep — I've told you it's a dangerous habit.'

But even Lady Constance subsided at Lord Alfred's fearsome frown which plainly stated who was still head of Mountford Hall.

'Come here, Emily. You were a brave child to risk your own life for an old man's. I've not much of mine left, but you've given me some more time.'

He leaned forward as she shyly edged a little nearer the bed. Such a pretty, slim, young thing. There was something about her, too. Ever since his wife, Sylvia, had died he thought more and more of that other poor, young girl — so long ago it seemed!

After he'd married he'd practically forgotten about it, especially when he and Lady Sylvia had lived abroad so happily. It was when he'd come back to the Hall alone — he couldn't get it out of his mind — never would, it seemed now, until he was dead and buried. He picked up an envelope from the bed.

'Here, Emily, is a token of my gratitude — take it.'

'Sir — I don't want . . . '

'Go on. I'm sure your family will be glad of some extra money. You've earned it!'

He waved it at her, and she took it reluctantly.

'Your hands — they're still bandaged. How are they?'

'Much better, Sir. Dr Moss said to keep the dressings on for a while.'

'Mr Williams is giving her light work only,' Lady Constance snapped out.

Lord Alfred pointedly ignored her.

'You live in Treskillen, Emily? Perhaps you should go home for a few days' holiday. Your mother would be glad to care for you.'

'I don't have a home, Sir. Since my father and brothers died . . . '

'I knew your father, George Trembarth. An . . . an unusual man. You and your mother will miss him.'

'We do.'

Emily felt a lump rise in her throat, and turned to go, but the old man put out a hand.'

'No — stay. I want to ask you . . . Your family, the Trembarths, were my tenants. I gave orders that no-one should be evicted because of the tragedy. Why did you leave?'

'No-one evicted us, Sir. My mother and sister, Polly, went to Plymouth. Mother couldn't settle after Father and the boys died.'

'Why Plymouth? What's there for her?'

'Her elder sister, my Aunt Maud, and Uncle Will have a guest house there. Polly goes to school, and Mother lends a hand with the visitors.'

'And where is this . . . guest house? In the town itself?'

'Near to the harbour, I believe, Sir.'

Emily wondered at Sir Alfred's interest in her family. Emily wondered if the old man was deliberately annoying his daughter-in-law by unsuitably chatting with the servants!

'And your Aunt Maud? Was she from Treskillen originally?'

'Oh, no, Sir. Auntie Maud's from

79

Devon. So was my mother. The Penroses were farmers on the Edgedown Estate, though many of their family emigrated to America.'

Emily stopped in alarm. Sir Alfred had slumped back against the pillows. Constance leaped up.

'Now look. I told you, Father-in-law, you've tired yourself.'

Sir Alfred opened his eyes and struggled to lean forward.

'No . . . no . . . I must talk to Emily again. Don't interfere, Constance. But I am tired just now. I'll send for you tomorrow, Emily and perhaps, when I'm feeling more able, you can wheel me around the grounds in that confounded bath-chair. I'd like that. I'll speak to Mr Williams . . . '

He fell back exhausted. But that name! He shuddered — Penrose, a common enough Devon name — a coincidence? It had to be. This girl would know nothing of the matter. It had all been hushed up very efficiently, so long ago.

'Come again, Emily,' he said tiredly, 'I want to sleep now.'

But it wasn't sleep he needed. Alfred Mountford wanted to force his mind back again, back sixty years — to the time when he was a fresh-faced young boy just home from his first term at public school, eager to tell his family all about his new school, eager especially, to tell his idolised older brother, Tom, all his news. But he never saw Tom — ever again — and life at Mountford Hall that Christmas holiday had been unbearable.

5

'Ralph! You must do something about that girl. Do you hear me? The Trembarth girl — you must dismiss her at once. Now! Stop looking at those papers and listen to me.'

Sir Ralph Mountford did not lift his head from the document he was studying. After a thorough perusal of the papers he picked a pen from the inkstand and slowly signed his name. When he'd completed the task to his satisfaction he looked up to face his angry wife.

'Constance, when I'm working on estate business you know I hate interruptions. Pray calm yourself. I shall be free this afternoon to discuss any problems you have with the staff.'

His wife fretted impatiently, hardly hearing him, her foot tapping with frustration. 'Mountford Hall has been nothing but trouble, especially since your father decided to resume nominal control of the estate after all those years abroad. You do all the work anyway.'

'Constance! That's enough. If you're not happy here, you have a choice.'

'What choice? I cannot return permanently to London without you.'

'And I choose to remain here. There's nothing more to say.'

'Ralph! It's the Trembarth girl I wish to speak of, not the question of where we make our permanent home. I'm concerned about your father.'

'He seems rather better in health and spirits lately.'

Constance's lips thinned, but she waited a second before laying an arm round her husband's shoulder. How she longed to return to London, but it was impossible until this problem was tackled. She softened her voice, massaged Sir Ralph's shoulder, and gradually his attention was caught.

'I'm merely concerned about your father. He's being a fool over the

83

Trembarth girl. Williams tells me the servants are starting to gossip. Lord Alfred singles her out for so much attention. Five times this week he's asked for her to wheel him about the grounds. Williams tells me Jacob is very put out. Unrest spreads so easily amongst servants.'

'Gossip? What sort of gossip?'

'They're saying there's no fool like an old fool, and your father is behaving like a fool over Emily Trembarth.'

Sir Ralph laid down his pen. Like father like son, he thought grimly. Constance was half his age, yet he could still recall how she'd captivated him on one of his business trips to London. He knew she found Cornwall dull, especially in the winter when London visitors were reluctant to brave the long journey. He relaxed under her soothing fingers and spoke mildly.

'There is surely no harm in the girl pushing father's bath chair around the rose garden? Her hands are still tender from the fire, and don't forget she pulled him from it — just in time. Father's grateful, that's all. The jealous gossip will die away when Emily returns to her normal duties.'

'But will she?'

'Constance! If you feel so strongly — well, dismiss the girl yourself. Now, if I may finish this farm inventory, I will see you at luncheon.'

Lady Constance all but stamped her foot.

'That is the problem, Ralph. I did dismiss her — and your father instantly countermanded my order. He absolutely refuses to let her go. I've been made to look a fool before the servants and that girl is crowing in triumph over me. It's intolerable.'

Sir Ralph turned to face his wife and thought for a few seconds.

'I suppose that does put you in a difficult situation. I'll speak to Father, but if he wishes the girl to stay there's little I can do.'

'Speak to him? You must do more than that. You must insist. Can't you see what the girl's up to? She's insinuating herself into your father's favour. Do you want to see her as mistress of Mountford Hall?'

'You go too far — and it's ridiculous. Ridiculous and spiteful. Go for a gallop on Firefly to get such wicked thoughts out of your system. I'm ashamed of you. I shall take luncheon with Father — you may please yourself. But I want to hear no more of this nonsensical notion of yours concerning my father.'

Outside the study door, Lady Constance clenched her fists, but she knew she'd pushed her husband too far. He'd never spoken to her like that. It was the girl's fault. Cornwall . . . Mountford Hall . . . tedious enough to drive her mad, and ever since the old man had set eyes on that parlour maid the place had been unbearable.

The longer the Trembarth girl stayed on at the all the more it became an obsession for Constance to sack her. She was determined to be rid of her by whatever means, but the old man was adamant and her husband was unlikely to be of much help.

She spent the rest of the morning telephoning her London friends. It was a chance remark from Cicely Westerridge that put an idea into her head. Immediately Cicely rang off, Constance Mountford asked the operator to connect her with Noah Templeton's law office in Exeter.

★ ★ ★

Lord Alfred motioned Emily to stop the chair by the rose garden. Leaning forward he touched the soft crimson petals.

'Such benign flowers, roses. See, still in full bloom so late in the year. These will flower almost until Christmas, though I doubt I'll see them.'

'Are you going away, Sir? Leaving Mountford Hall?'

'Should you mind, Emily, if I did leave?'

'I . . . I don't know, Sir. You've been

so kind to me . . . '

She would have preferred to leave when Lady Constance sacked her a few weeks after the fire. Harry had been delighted, sure she'd return to Treskillen and marry him. But Lord Alfred had peremptorily countermanded his daughter-in-law's instructions and had personally requested Emily to stay on at Mountford Hall. He'd also increased her wages. The chill frostiness of Lady Constance's demeanour became worse.

Nor did Emily have much support below stairs. Jacob was particularly jealous and made his views clear to the rest.

' 'Tain't parlourmaid's job to wheel His Lordship. 'Tis mine — or I shouldn't mind James doing it when he's not chauffeuring m'Lady.'

Only Lord Alfred's insistence she stay kept her from leaving the Hall, but her days must be running out and she'd already written to her mother in Plymouth asking about jobs there, shelving yet again a decision about Harry. Meanwhile, she made the best of things.

Blow them all, she thought as she pushed the invalid chair carefully around the formal gardens. What other chance would she ever get to hear such interesting things from a man like Lord Alfred? His description of all the places in the world he'd visited held her so enthralled she could forget the petty jealousies of her fellow servants.

'Wheel the chair to the summerhouse, Emily, by the lake. I instructed Williams to put coffee there. The wind's getting a little chilly now.'

'Would you prefer me to take you back to the house, Sir?'

'No, not just yet. The sun's strong out of the wind, and it's sheltered by the lake. I'd like to see the swans.'

'Very well.'

Coffee was set on a rustic table inside the summerhouse. There were two cups, a silver flask, and a covered plate of biscuits. Emily settled Lord

Alfred by the table where he could see the stately swans gliding among the rushes then stood to one side whilst he poured coffee, adding a splash of brandy to one of the drinks. She wondered who the second cup was for.

'Sit down — drink your coffee while it's hot,' Lord Alfred said.

'Sir, I don't think Mr Williams . . .'

'Be hanged to Mr Williams. I don't take orders from Williams.'

'Sir, I appreciate your kindness to me, and I hope you won't take offence at what I say . . .'

'Well, well, what is it? I shan't bite you, you should know that by now.'

'Sir, I do have to take my orders from Mr Williams, and the others below stairs are wondering why you pick on me to be your wheel-chair attendant. Not that I don't like it — I do.'

He looked at her intently before he answered.

'I expect they do wonder,' he said

thoughtfully. 'I tell you, Emily, I have a reason — and that you will hear soon enough, when I'm ready. Until then the rest of them can mind their business. Has anyone been unkind to you?'

'Oh, no, Sir,' Emily lied, thinking that Lady Constance's glacial manner and nasty remarks weren't the end of the world.

'Drink your coffee then, have a biscuit, and sit down.'

Emily did as she was told and there was silence — calm and companionable between them.

'That's better,' Lord Alfred said quietly. 'Now, talk to me of Treskillen and what you used to do there.'

Lord Alfred always made her feel at ease — almost an equal. It was a good feeling.

'You know most of it, Sir — that I used to fish with my dad and brothers. But I didn't tell you about the Huer's Stone. I used to watch out for the pilchard shoals coming in, just as my grandfather did. He taught me . . . '

'Will Trembarth. Of course! I'd forgotten. D'you know, Emily, I sometimes would go to Treskillen with the Estate Manager when I was a little boy . . . so long ago.'

'You knew my grandfather!'

'I remember a young lad by the Stone — told me his name was Will Trembarth. Told me about the pilchards, too. I recall it clearly. I'd dearly love to see that view over the bay once more — stand on that stone overlooking the dark blue seas of Cornwall. Happy days, Emily . . . before . . .'

He stopped and the light faded from his eyes.

'Sir, you could go, in the motor car. The path'll take a motor right up by the Stone.'

'I will go. You shall come with me. Soon.'

'But . . . Lady Constance . . . '

'Leave that to me.'

His tone was so stern she dare not protest.

More gently, he asked, 'Do you miss Treskillen?'

'I do, Sir. Yes.'

'You have a young man there? Someone to make a home with?'

'Well, sort of, but I'm not sure about living in Treskillen for ever. I used to think that's all I ever wanted, but since I've been at the Hall, I've thought maybe there are other things to do, to see. Do you know, Lord Alfred, I've never been out of Cornwall, and if I marry Harry, perhaps I never shall. I never thought I should want to leave Cornwall, but listening to you, all the countries you've visited . . . America . . . Africa . . . well . . . '

He smiled, and for one fleeting moment she glimpsed the young man behind the lined, old face. Then the sadness returned and there was the old man again — one very near the end of his journey. He looked so desolate, Emily longed to take his hand in comfort, but the class lines were still too deep-drawn between them for such a gesture on her part.

'I'm sorry, Sir. I didn't mean . . . '

'No, no. I like to hear your enthusiasm. Go after your dreams, Emily. Life's too soon done. You should take your opportunities. The times are changing and you must change with them. You're so young.'

Chance would be a fine thing, Emily thought as she tidied up the cups, but all she said was, 'It's not so easy, Sir, to leave my roots.'

She made to release the brake on the wheel-chair, but he stayed her hand. His next words were laboured, as though he forced himself to speak.

'Tell me about your roots . . . your mother's family. Penrose, you said?'

She nodded. 'I know little of them. My Penrose grandparents died when mother was just a baby. Auntie Maud, the one in Plymouth, brought up the family, then when Mother married there was some sort of disagreement. I never knew what it was. Aunt Maud never came to Treskillen, until the funeral. I think it saddened Mother. That's why she was happy to go to Plymouth with Maud, pay the debt she owed, she said.'

'And were there others . . . brothers, sisters, your aunts and uncles?'

'None that I know myself, Sir. I believe I have uncles in America, with their own families by now if they're still alive. I should like to find out one day — if I ever get the chance.'

'No aunts then, apart from Maud?'

'I don't think so. Mother only spoke of Maud, and that rarely until lately. I hardly know a thing about the Penrose side. I suppose I should ask my mother. I will, when I go to visit. It's important, Sir, isn't it, to know about your family, the background . . .'

She jumped up quickly. Lord Alfred was so still, so white, she was alarmed.

'Are you all right, Sir? I think we'd better go back.'

He started. 'Yes. All right, Emily. I am . . . suddenly . . . very tired.'

Emily wheeled him back as fast as

she could, worried by his ashen colour, anxious to get him indoors. As she turned the corner by the rose garden the rug slipped and became entangled in the wheels.

As she kneeled to retrieve it, Lord Alfred caught her hand in a grip, the strength of which surprised her. He leaned forward and searched her face as though looking for the answer to something. They remained so for long seconds. He released her with a sigh.

'Emily Trembarth, I'm sorry, sorrier than I can ever tell you.'

'For what, Sir? You've been nothing but kind to me.'

'I'm glad of that . . .'

He closed his eyes and slumped back in his chair. Emily tucked the rug around him and began to push him up the drive. Then fear made her heart skip a beat as she saw Lady Constance on the front steps, Jacob behind her, jealous dislike in his eyes. But it was hatred and something akin to envy that flared in Lady Constance's eyes. Her tongue was whiplash.

'You've kept Lord Alfred out too long. What do you think you are doing? He looks ill. Do you intend him to catch a chill? Jacob, take the chair at once into the house, and you, miss, return to your proper place by the servants' entrance.'

Jacob ran down the steps, picked up man and chair as though it were a baby carriage, and carried them into the house without a glance at Emily. The door slammed, leaving her standing on the gravel below, with a deep and dreadful sense of foreboding in her soul.

6

Noah Templeton eyed Lady Constance with suspicion. She was putting on an act, he was sure. It wasn't her usual style to be so flatteringly attentive to a country lawyer, even though his law firm was directly connected to the London solicitors who dealt with the main Mountford estate business.

'You will stay for lunch, Noah? I would value your opinion on a new hunter I'm thinking of buying. Cicely told me you are so knowledgeable about horseflesh. Sherry — before lunch?'

'A small one. I'd be delighted to advise you, although Miss Westerridge's opinion of me seems somewhat inflated.'

'Such a vivacious girl — and very well connected.'

'A business matter you said on the telephone?' Noah deflected Lady Constance. 'I do need to return to

Exeter today — as soon as I've seen Lord Alfred, or Ralph. I assume it's a matter concerning the estate. Lord Alfred is well?'

'Confined to bed. A chill,' Lady Constance said rather dryly.

'I'm sorry to hear it. May I see him?'

'I'd rather not disturb him at present. He's very feverish. And Ralph's in London on business.'

Noah frowned. What on earth was she up to? It had been a tedious journey from Plymouth that morning, and he had little time for a wild goose-chase based on a whim of Lady Constance.

'It is I who need your help and advice. This is a little difficult for me, but I feel I cannot allow the situation to continue.'

'Situation? What situation? Please come to the point, Constance.'

'The business is very much to do with Lord Alfred . . . and the estate. You must help me.'

'If you would explain.'

'You are fond of His Lordship?'

'Of course. I have known him since I was a boy.'

'So you would not want him to come to any harm, or do anything he may regret — in his dotage?'

'Naturally not, but I am at a loss to imagine where all this is leading.'

'I very much fear that Lord Alfred is about to make a fool of himself.'

'The point, please, Constance.'

'It's that girl. Emily Trembarth!'

'Emily? What . . . ?'

'His Lordship appears very taken with her as a . . . a . . . companion. Constantly calls for her to wheel him out, or to read to him, or even sit with him by the library fire while he takes his meals in there. He insists she serve him herself — the next thing she will be dining with him! It must be stopped. I know your philosophy tends to the radical but even you can see that she must be stopped . . . . before irreparable damage is caused.'

'Damage? What can you mean?'

'I fear the worst. My father-in-law may be so besotted as to ask her to become his wife. I've tried to dismiss her but Lord Alfred won't hear of it. You must use your influence.'

'How can I? I've no influence. This is not estate business. And I'm sure you're quite mistaken about His Lordship's intentions.'

'She's a schemer, a hussy! Why, the other day she kept him out in the grounds so long he caught a feverish chill. I've had a hard time keeping her out of the sick-room. Lord Alfred constantly asks for her but the doctor fortunately commanded complete rest.'

'But it's absurd. I'm sure you'll find Lord Alfred is merely taking a kindly interest in an employee — one who saved his life, don't forget.'

'Am I ever allowed to forget that? The affair must be stopped. We shall be the laughing stock of the county. As for London — should it become known there . . . ' A shudder ran through her body. It was unthinkable.

Noah put his glass on a side table. 'Thank you for the sherry. Perhaps another time we can discuss your new hunter. I really do have to return to Exeter today. As for the notion that Emily Trembarth is scheming to become mistress of Mountford Hall, I can assure you your fears are groundless. Miss Trembarth has a young man, a Treskillen fisherman — and how could I help you even if she was planning such a coup?'

Constance's look was stormy. How could a simple fisherman compete with the huge wealth and status of Lord Alfred Mountford. In Constance's world women sought the highest bidder. She was not going to see her chance of joining the nobility snatched by a young parlour-maid who might jeopardise her own husband's position.

'Please, Noah, talk to the girl. You seem able to get along with people of her class. Persuade her to leave Mountford Hall of her own accord whilst Lord Alfred is still feverish. When he's recovered and she's gone, perhaps he will come to his senses. He could hardly chase her to Treskillen.'

'I'm sorry, Constance, but I can't take this seriously. Of course I can't interfere. Now, if you'll excuse me . . . '

'Wait!' Her sharp command stopped him at the door. 'Then my alternative is to over-ride Lord Alfred and dismiss her, but I shall inform both her mother and this fisherman of her conduct in this house. She will never obtain another post, and even if she returns to Treskillen I shall make known her despicable intentions so she will find it hard to live there comfortably. I shall personally see to it that the girl's reputation is ruined.'

'You mean that?'

'Unless you talk to her, persuade her to leave here of her own free will. Threaten her with the law if necessary . . . '

Noah shook his head in stunned disbelief. He recalled Emily's pretty, animated young face by the Huer's Stone, her young man's possessive embrace, her bravery on the morning of the fire. He'd wager his life she was no schemer. Lady Constance was the dangerous one! Emily Trembarth was no match for the aristocratic Lady Constance Mountford. The girl would be ruined. He felt surging anger.

The best plan for Emily would be to get away from the Hall as soon as possible — back to her fisherman. That prospect curiously brought scant pleasure to Noah, but he knew he must help her.

He looked coldly at Lady Constance.

'I will speak to Miss Trembarth, but understand this, it is as a favour to the girl herself, not to assist you in your unbecoming conduct.'

She scowled but held her peace. Once Noah Templeton had used whatever influence he had with the servant girl he could return to Exeter for good as far as she was concerned. Frostily, she inclined her head.

'As you wish. I instructed Williams to make sure the girl would be in the housekeeper's sitting-room at this time. You will be alone with her there.'

Noah strode furiously down the corridors to the servants' quarters and vowed he'd never set foot in the place again. In spite of his liking for Lord Alfred and Ralph, he couldn't stomach another encounter with the mistress of Mountford Hall.

'What the hang am I going to say to Emily Trembarth,' he muttered to himself as Williams ushered him into Mrs Miller's private sitting room.

Emily was darning pillow-cases, not a task she enjoyed. The room was close and stuffy, the pile of sheets and towels never-ending. She had been more-or-less sent to Coventry by the downstairs staff. Only Clarrie and Martha had a kind word for her. She'd been blamed for Lord Alfred's illness, Lady Constance's evil temper, and Sir Ralph's bolt to London!

Since coffee in the summerhouse,

the Master of Mountford had been confined to his bedroom and there was no word for her as to his progress. It was only her concern for him that kept her there. The moment she heard news of his improved health she would leave.

But her problem was where to go? Her mother had written that there was no work in Plymouth at present, with the summer ended. Sarah Trembarth wrote that Emily was well off at Mountford Hall, and should remain there. Meanwhile, she and Polly missed her. Small consolation, Emily thought, and Harry had not visited the Hall for over two weeks!

The knock startled her.

'Come in . . . Mrs Miller's not . . . Mr Templeton!' Her spirits lifted as she rose to greet him.

'Miss Trembarth,' he replied gravely. 'I see you're busy.'

Emily pulled a face. He noted she was pale. Her hair, drawn back under the frilled cap, lacked its usual lustre.

'Sit down, Emily, it's you I came to see.'

Her leap of pleasure was stifled by apprehension. What could he want from her?

He pushed the linen to one side and sat by her. She looked so forlorn he took her hands and held them fast in spite of her attempts to draw away as she felt the warm pressure of his flesh. But the jolt of pleasure at seeing him disappeared. She remembered him dancing with that girl in the ballroom. She picked up her sewing and wished he'd tell her why he was there, then go.

'Leave the mending for a moment. I need to speak to you.'

'I'm not allowed to be idle. I'll sew as you speak.'

'You don't look as you did before, Emily, by the Huer's Stone, in the ballroom the night before the fire. You had a sparkle . . . a zest for excitement. It's gone. Aren't you happy here?'

She bit off a piece of thread and Noah saw her soft lips tremble against even white teeth.

'I don't suppose you've ever been a servant, Mr Templeton. You'll have no notion of what it's like to live happy or miserable, dependant on an employer's whim or mood. A bad day for master or mistress can result in a week's despondency for the servant. We may not indulge our dreams or have opinions of our own if it doesn't suit our superiors.'

'You're right, I've never been in that servitude, nor do I like to see any human being chained in subservience to another if he wished not to be so. Surely you are free to leave here if you are so unhappy. You have a young man in Treskillen . . . '

'If I have, that is my affair. I'm sure you mean well, sir, but you have no right to question me about my personal life. Lord Alfred wishes me to stay at the Hall. He, at least, has been very kind to me and it would be ungrateful to go against his wishes. Do you know how he is, sir?'

'There is no need to call me sir, Emily. Lady Constance tells me Lord Alfred is still feverish.'

'You've not seen him?'

'No.'

'No-one will tell me. They all blame me for his chill, but I wouldn't harm him for the world.'

Emily was confused by Noah's stare, probing, even accusing. What had she done? He distracted her.

'I shan't always be a servant here,' she burst out defiantly.

'I never thought that was your intention.'

'Since the fire, Lord Alfred has talked to me of other countries, other lives ... America, where there are opportunities — no need for servants.'

'His Lordship talks to you a lot?'

'Why shouldn't he? I wheel his chair around the grounds. Am I supposed to be a deaf mute?'

'Calm yourself ... such agitation ... '

Yet anger suited her. Defiance had enlivened her being, pride stiffened her. He should have realised Constance's message was inappropriate, and he had no taste for being her messenger. Emily Trembarth had spirit enough to make her own way.

'I see we are destined to be at cross purposes, Miss Trembarth. Here is my card . . . if ever you do need any help . . . you or your young man . . . '

'Thank you, Mr Templeton, but I believe Lord Alfred will look after me. Just as soon as he's recovered from this chill I mean to . . . '

She stopped. What did it matter to Noah Templeton what she planned to do? How could he possibly be interested? He was a friend of Lady Constance, and she'd probably sent him especially to taunt her.

'When Lord Alfred recovers . . . ?' he queried, to prompt her further.

'I mean not to be a parlour-maid at Mountford Hall, you can be certain of that. I'll do anything . . . '

Noah's hands grasped her shoulders, his fingers digging into her flesh. His eyes were contemptuous, his voice harsh.

'You disappoint me, Emily Trembarth. I thought better of you.'

He released her so suddenly she staggered, but he left the room without a backward glance, failing to see the look of bewilderment on Emily's face.

Noah was startled by the strength of his emotions as he made his way back to the main house. Anger at himself for bungling the talk with Emily, fury with Constance, and a curious ambivalence concerning Lord Alfred and Emily. Could there really be anything in Constance's wild fantasy?

Emily reminded him of a trapped deer at bay — one who'd take any course to spring the trap — but marriage to Lord Alfred? In spite of his liberal views, he knew it would be a disaster for Emily.

In the main hall, he paused. There was no sign of Williams or Jacob.

The house was quiet. A sense of unfinished business sent him upstairs in the direction of Lord Alfred's rooms. After all, that was his original intention in visiting the Mountford Estate.

Less than an hour later he left the Hall, his brain whirling with speculation about the contents of the large envelope Lord Alfred had made him promise to send by special delivery. The address was a familiar one — the London parent company of his own firm of solicitors in Exeter — but the envelope was marked Highly Confidential, and Lord Alfred had not disclosed the contents to Noah. He had also asked Noah to telephone Ralph — urgently!

7

Noah's cold anger at the end of their encounter unsettled Emily. Nothing was going right at Mountford Hall. Whatever the future held she could no longer endure the present situation. The decision made, she sought out Mr Williams.

'Very wise, to leave of your own free will. Your work at least has been satisfactory. I shall happily supply a reference should you wish.'

Williams' habit of discretion was so ingrained, tact was part of his nature. No-one had ever questioned Emily's capacity for cheerful hard work. Nevertheless he was pleased to report her resignation to Lady Constance.

'Excellent news indeed. Pay the girl wages in lieu of notice. She can go tomorrow. Her sort are always trouble.'

'There is a little problem m'lady.

Emily has no prospect . . . '

'Her problem, not ours.'

'Not quite, Madam. Sir Ralph telephoned while you were out riding. He is returning from London this evening with a party of business associates.'

'Business associates?'

Lady Constance frowned. Unusual! Ralph hated entertaining, and never initiated it. What a prospect — stuffy middle-aged bores. But at least Noah had solved her problem. She forgot her animosity towards him and remembered how attractive he was. Perhaps he could join the party at some point.

'Er . . . and their wives, Madam.'

'Wives! Ah! The business wives — you have a list of names, Williams?'

'Yes m'lady . . . several names are familiar guests.'

'That's a relief. But if you need extra help, surely there is someone from the village.'

'With respect, we employ most of the suitable girls. It is short notice, and Mrs Miller is not due to return

114

from her sister's until late tomorrow.'

'Oh, very well, let the girl stay a day or so, but the moment you can manage — she goes.'

'Yes, Madam.'

Although Emily was as anxious to leave as Lady Constance was to be rid of her, another few days at the Hall gave her a respite to think of the future. Plymouth? Treskillen? Then a daring thought — why not America?

As soon as the staff heard Emily was leaving, hostility abated and for two days Emily was happy enough. The house was overflowing and Lady Constance was delighted to find several of the younger women smart sophisticated company. With Lord Alfred confined to bed, and the girl leaving at any moment, she considered she'd won. The affair was closed.

On the third day, Sir Ralph arranged a moorland shoot. Williams was instructed to supply a large picnic luncheon. The ladies were to form a complementary sketching party. One of London's leading entrepreneurs had promised a prize for the best Cornish water colour.

The men left in a dawn mist, the women followed more leisurely when the sun was well up. Jacob and James were to take the two cars and the hampers to the picnic site for mid-day.

Clarrie and Emily were packing pies into a box when the bell from Lord Alfred's rooms jangled. Mr Williams rolled down his shirt sleeves and buttoned his jacket. He was the only person allowed to answer the bell.

'Is Lord Alfred better now?' Emily dared ask.

'Improving, I believe, though Dr Moss calls daily.'

His tone discouraged further questions and Emily turned back to the pies. She would like to have seen him just once more before she left.

Ten minutes later, Mr Williams, unusually agitated, returned to the hall.

'Where's James?' he asked.

'Out by the motor, about to set off,' Clarrie answered.

'Run and stop him. No, not you, Emily, you stay where you are.'

Emily's sense of foreboding returned. There was something wrong! Why was he looking at her so strangely? Acting so nervously?

'Anything wrong, Sir. Lord Alfred . . . ?' she asked.

The bell jangled again as James sauntered back into the hall.

'What's up with that danged bell? Stuck is it?'

'Lord Alfred wants you now. The bell won't stop until you get there. His Lordship wants to go out. You're to drive him and . . . and . . . '

'Car's already packed for the picnic,' James interrupted.

'Well unpack it. He's in no mood to be thwarted, I can tell you . . . and, Emily, you're to go as well.'

'Me? What . . . ?'

'Don't ask. I just wish Sir Ralph was here.'

'Don't worry, I shan't go, Sir.'

'You have no choice. Lord Alfred is adamant. James — quick, get along. We'll unpack the car, you see to His Lordship. Bring him down to the front entrance, and you'd better put the wheel-chair in. Heaven knows what he's up to. Let's pray it's all over with before Lady Constance returns. Emily, look sharp. Jacob, you drive the motor round to the front to meet James.'

The car was quickly emptied, and Emily climbed in beside a stoney-faced Jacob.

As they drew up at the entrance, Lord Alfred, muffled in dark coat, scarf and hat, looking so frail and ill, smiled when he saw Emily.

'Sir,' she ran up the steps, 'are you well enough to be out?'

'Yes, I am. I've plotted for this. The cats are away, so I'm escaping. Virtually imprisoned in my own home. Asked for you several times.'

'I didn't know.'

'Humph! I see — confirms my

conspiracy theory. Never mind, now's our chance. Off you go, Jacob. You can get over to the picnic now. Get in, my dear. No, not in the front with James — in the back with me. James'll drive us. Go on, Jacob, your face is enough to put the sun out, and I want to stay warm. We're going to the Huer's Stone, Emily, just as I promised.'

He tapped James on the shoulder with his cane.

'Towards Treskillen, then Emily'll direct you.'

He slid shut the glass panel separating driver from passengers and leaned back with a satisfied smile.

'I'm enjoying this. My daughter-in-law thought she could keep me locked up. Devil's own job till young Templeton appeared out of the blue. I used him as a courier — sent out my messages. I know what's going on, Emily. I may be old but the brain still works, and I've had more time than I need to think lately. Noah got in touch with Ralph who did as instructed for once. Drummed up a house party — plenty of distraction — no-one to worry about me. So here we are — on our way to the Huer's Stone. We'll stop on the way and buy our own picnic.'

'I hope you won't over-tax yourself, Sir.'

Emily was worried. Excitement danced in Lord Alfred's eyes, but his skin was paper-thin, breathing seemed an effort, and his hands shook.

'Don't fret. I take full responsibility. You've nothing to worry about. I know you're leaving. I'm sorry, but it's right that you should do so now. And it's time to explain my special interest in your family. I like to think there's a happy bond between Mountfords and Trembarths. Oh, I know your father was a rebel, but he was a good fellow. The other side of your family, the Penroses, is a different matter and we have much to make amends for.'

'I don't know what you mean, Sir. How can . . . ?'

'Patience, Emily. I want to enjoy our

day out, not cloud it at the outset with darker memories.'

Emily saw the exertion of speaking had tired him. His initial burst of energy was fading. He took her hand and held it as though drawing strength from her youth to get him through the day, and she let it lie within his clasp. Once, he slid back the panel and gave orders for James to stop at an inn.

'Something simple, bread, cheese, or pasties.' He chuckled. 'And champagne, if they have it! You ever had champagne, Emily?'

'No, Sir.'

Emily felt she was living a dream. The narrow, high-hedged lanes twisted and turned towards the coast. When they finally reached the Huer's Stone. Emily felt a loving sense of familiar homecoming. She was glad the cliff top was deserted. It would be hard to explain to any passer-by from the village why she was sitting in the back of the smart motor, sipping champagne with Lord Mountford — especially as she couldn't explain it herself!

Lord Alfred was silent as he looked out of the window. Granite cliffs rose majestically like protecting sentinels around the sweep of dark water.

'A fine sight. I'd forgotten. So many years ago I sat on that stone with Will Trembarth . . . all the countries in the world and this is on my own doorstep. You know, Emily, we take our own backyards too much for granted. I should have come back sooner.'

'At least you've seen other back gardens, Sir.'

'True. And you'd like to?'

'I think I might now. Yet, I'd always come back here. I'd like to be out there in the bay, fishing, right now.'

'Maybe, one day, Emily, you'll follow all your dreams. James, I'll get out of the motor for a while — feel the sun. Don't fuss, Emily, I'm well muffled.'

He looked at her anxious face and smiled. Such a pretty young girl — if the other one had looked so . . . He could understand now, the temptation, eyes like hedgerow bluebells, such a waist, an air of innocence, and yet, he was sure, a steely spirit somewhere there. He hoped so — she'd need it! He sighed and turned back to the sea. This was his farewell to Treskillen Bay, he knew that.

'Emily, I'd like to see you on the Stone, watching for the pilchards like Will did. James, the wheel-chair, I think.'

He was alarmed at the way his legs buckled under him as he stepped out of the motor. James placed the chair on the path and, a little self-consciously, Emily climbed up the steps to the platform.

'Tell me what you see, Emily.'

'The sea's flat calm, deep, deep blue today. Darker patches by the rocks. Not pilchards, that season's over, but fishing boats are quite far out. The gulls are wheeling round the boats — they'll be gutting out the catch. Harry will be there with his new boat.

It's just like it used to be . . . before the accident.'

'I can't see the boats. Wheel me a little nearer.'

'No, wait, sir. You're too close to the edge . . . James . . . '

Emily screamed as Lord Alfred's chair jolted forward as he half rose. For a nightmare second it teetered on the brink of tipping up and depositing him perilously near the cliff edge, but she leaped down from the Stone, snatched the handle, and threw her weight against the chair and man. She felt him gasp, then James was helping her pull them back to the car.

'Sir, you gave me a fright. I thought you'd topple into the sea.'

'Unlikely. I'm not quite ready to go over the top yet. What the devil . . . '

Emily looked up. There was another motor car lurching along the narrow track and she recognised it as the one Jacob drove to the picnic. In the back seat, fury personified, was Lady Constance Mountford.

'Damn!' Lord Alfred ground out. 'Damn the woman. Am I not to be left in peace? Don't be alarmed, Emily, this expedition was entirely of my making.'

He greeted her as she leaped out of the car, hardly waiting until it had halted.

'Constance, what are you doing here? Don't you have Ralph's guests to consider? The picnic lunch?'

'What do you think you're doing. You're an invalid — feverish.'

'Bah! A slight chill. You made it out much worse than it was. The day will never arrive, Constance, when you dictate my actions. The drive has done me good. Miss Trembarth and James have been model nursemaids. Go back to your guests and leave me to enjoy the rest of the day in peace.'

'It's that girl, isn't it? She schemed and plotted to get you out of the house. She should have left the Hall days ago. How dare you take my father-in-law from his sick bed and bring him out here. It's positively dangerous, so close to the cliff edge. What Sir Ralph will say . . . '

'Ralph has more sense than to say anything about such a minor matter. You are making a fool of yourself, Constance, and spoiling Ralph's party. Jacob, turn round and drive Her Ladyship back to the picnic at once.'

'I'd prefer it if you came back to the house with me, Father-in-law. James can follow — and I propose to leave this girl in her native village. Doubtless someone will give her a bed for the night. Williams will see her things are sent here. I will not have her at Mountford Hall.'

'Don't you dare dictate to me as to what will become of Miss Trembarth. She returns with me. I have something to say to her, so I ask you, for the last time, to leave. I shall finish this day as I started it.'

She had no choice but to back down and obey.

'Very well. But if that girl does not

leave tomorrow, I won't answer for the consequences.'

Emily thought it was high time she asserted her point of view.

'I was intending to leave first thing tomorrow — and I should be quite happy to be left here in Treskillen.'

'No!' Lord Alfred quelled her with a look. 'You will return with me, and you will leave in an appropriate and proper manner tomorrow. Constance, I warn you, Emily is now answerable only to me.'

Lady Constance bent her head, before climbing, stiff-backed, into the car. As the motor disappeared down the track, Lord Alfred sat back in his chair and beckoned James.

'Help me into the car now. Emily, I should have liked to visit the village, meet your young man, see the cottage where your family lived, but I find myself more exhausted than I thought.'

Damn Constance, he thought, she'd drained his energy. The Huer's Stone was to have been symbolic — where he'd intended to begin to right the wrong before living memory of it was lost. He leaned back. Perhaps it had been a foolish whim, but at least he'd seen Treskillen Bay.

As the luxurious motor purred quietly back along the lanes, Lord Alfred began to speak.

'Emily, I have to tell you . . . since my dear wife died, I've been burdened. While she was alive we were so happy . . . I never thought. Selfish! Mountford Hall, when we lived abroad, was another world. But there's something I have to tell you . . . '

'Please, Lord Alfred, not now. Rest now.'

'No. I can't die until I've put right the wrong to your family.'

Her voice broke with fear as Lord Alfred, with laboured breathing, clutched his heart.

'Sir — Lord Alfred — you're ill.' She rapped the panel behind the chauffeur. 'James, pull up.'

'No,' Lord Alfred gasped. 'There are

pills in my pocket . . . here . . . water
in that flask.'

He pulled out a phial and Emily
quickly shook out the pills. He nodded,
swallowed them and seized the flask
from her. James's eyes, in the mirror,
were wide and worried.

'Shall I stop the car, Sir?' he called
back.

'For a moment, yes. The pills work
quickly.'

James pulled into a farm entrance
and turned off the engine, springing
out of the driver's seat.

Lord Alfred lay back against the
upholstery, eyes closed, but already
his breathing was easier. He smiled
weakly.

'You were right, Emily, I am too
tired. Carry on, James. It's not far.'

Emily straightened the rug round his
knees and took the flask from him.

'Lord Alfred, please rest now. Whatever was in the past, I can't believe
it's that important. How could the
Mountfords have wronged my family?

I'm sure if they did, you've paid for it with your kindness to me. No, I'll not let you say another word. Close your eyes and try to sleep.'

'You're a good girl, Emily Trembarth. I'm glad you came to Mountford Hall. It was the shock I needed . . . to put it all right. The diaries . . . I'll finish tonight. You must come to say goodbye. There's a letter for your mother and Maud Broome — the Penrose girls.'

As soon as they arrived back at the Hall, Dr Moss was sent for. The house-guests returned from the moorland picnic and the grand finale dinner had to be attended to, baths to be heated, ladies coiffed and dressed.

Dr Moss was closeted with Sir Ralph.

'Your father's health is precarious and has been for some time. He has something on his mind which upsets him — to do with the Trembarth girl.'

'She leaves tomorrow.'

'If he wants to see her — he must. Agitation, any upset, could do him great harm. He needs rest and quiet. If Lady Constance . . . er . . .'

'I shall see to it my wife does not disturb my father.'

'I'll look in again and leave a sleeping draught. Make sure he has a good long sleep — the best restorative I know.'

During the small lull between dinner and late supper, Mr Williams drew Emily to one side.

'Lord Alfred wishes you to take up his hot milk before he settles for the night. I prefer the rest of the staff do not know. His Lordship wishes to say goodbye personally. I have prepared the milk myself. It's in the small pantry. Slip away and, Emily, only a few moments. His Lordship isn't to be upset.'

Music and laughter wafted from the library and dining-room as she tip-toed up the stairs. His sitting-room was empty but there was a soft sound from an adjoining room. The huge fire in the grate made the bedroom stuffy, far too hot, Emily thought as she carried the milk to the bedside.

'Emily? I'm glad you've come. I'm sorry if I gave you a fright — all that nonsense of an attack. I feel much better. Sit down — sit down.'

'I've come to say goodbye, Sir. Mr Williams said only for a moment.'

'Don't you remember what I said? You're in my employ. If you're going to be one of life's travellers you'll have to learn to stand up for yourself. I think you will learn. Now pop this powder in the milk. Dr Moss left it and I promised Ralph I'd take it after I'd spoken to you.'

She unfolded the paper, shook the powder into the warm liquid, and handed it to him. He drank it in one draught and settled back on his pillows.

'Sit down — on the chair by me where I can see you. There. Do you know, Emily, when I first saw you I'd been thinking more and more of that young girl. I was only ten or eleven years old, excited about going away to school. It was Tom's school, at least it had been. He was older than me and at Cambridge University. I'd so much looked forward to that Christmas. Tom was — such a man! I thought he was God!'

Emily sat quite still. What on earth was he talking about?

'But that Christmas, I found out my elder brother was no god! I arrived home in the middle of such a row with Tom and my father shouting, Mother crying, the servants creeping about. I couldn't understand it. No-one would talk to me. After all the shouting, Tom was so glum. I asked him what it was all about. He said I was too young and I should go off to bed. Well, Emily, I went — if they weren't interested in my news, I wouldn't tell them. I even wished I was back at school.'

'Lord Alfred, Sir, shouldn't you be sleeping?' Emily pleaded, wondering why on earth he was telling her all this.

'No, I'm comfortable.' His eyes were back in the past. 'Later, I heard visitors arrive. Nothing unusual there, but the shouting started again, men arguing, stamping — my father's voice above the rest. I crept out of my room to listen. I heard him order the people out of the house. Then, suddenly, a gun shot, a scream, and then awful silence. I stayed where I was until Tom found me. He was in a dreadful state, kept saying he had to go . . . sorry he'd spoiled my Christmas, hoped there'd be happier times . . . '

Emily hoped the draught would soon take effect, and couldn't see why he was telling her this rambling dream.

He lifted his head with an effort, his words breathing out.

'Those men who came that night . . . Jim Penrose, your other grandfather, Jabez and Michael, his sons, your uncles. Emily, my father . . . shot . . . your Uncle Jabez . . . ' His head fell back, and a soft sighing snore told Emily he was in a sound slumber.

She stayed a while, then straightened the bed covers, picked up the empty cup of milk, and crept quietly from the room.

8

Emily pleaded tiredness that night to evade Clarrie's persistent questioning about the day's events, but she lay wakeful for long hours afterwards. Her brain whirled with Lord Alfred's tantalising, unfinished story. Was it possible that Lord George Mountford, the stern-faced baronet who glared down the long picture gallery at his numerous ancestors, had shot her uncle, Jabez Penrose? She'd never heard of Jabez, or Michael, though her mother had never mentioned Will Penrose, her grandfather. Emily longed to hear the rest of the story.

Towards dawn she fell asleep, but was disturbed by noises — carriages, a car engine, voices. Restless, she woke at her usual hour. Her uniforms were washed and pressed, ready to leave behind for the next parlour maid, so she wore the Sunday best skirt and blouse she'd arrived in. The cart was due at ten o'clock, but she knew Lord Alfred would send for her before then. He couldn't leave the story unfinished!

Clarrie woke, dressed, and said sadly, 'I'll miss you — ' then she broke off as the door burst open.

The young maid, Martha, practically fell into the room.

'What's the matter? Calm down.' Emily put her arm around the weeping girl, who was doubled up, gasping for breath.

'The Master . . . Lord Alfred . . . he's dead!' she eventually blurted out.

'Dead? He can't be. I spoke to him last night,' Emily whispered. 'I had to take Lord Alfred's milk up. Mr Williams told me to.'

'Danged long time in there, you were, Jacob said. I never believed what he said before about you and His Lordship but now I . . . '

'He was only being kind to me . . . interested in my family. How could you possibly imagine . . . what could you think?'

Clarrie tossed her head and adjusted her cap and tied her apron strings more firmly.

' 'Twill be Lord Ralph now, I suppose. All the same to us — so long as wages are paid regular.'

'Don't you care at all about Lord Alfred?' Emily was shocked.

'Why ever should I? Hardly spoke two words to me — not like some! Come on, Martha, we can't sit here, idling the day away.'

Clarrie banged out of the room, pushing Martha before her.

In the silent attic room a sadness settled round Emily's heart. Dead! He'd been so kind — and she thought he'd liked her. It wasn't just for the strange connection between the families, she was certain of that. Now, she'd never know the end of the story, but her mother, or Aunt Maud at least, must know something!

It was to Plymouth, not Treskillen,

she must go. Now her protector had gone she must leave Mountford Hall at once, especially, if everyone thought that she and Lord Alfred . . . She burned with shameful anger at the thought. She had money enough to get to Plymouth.

There was no possible back way out except via the servants' hall, but Emily saw no reason to creep away like a criminal. She was no longer in the Mountford employ, so why not the front entrance?

She went through the green baize door, down the carpeted corridor, rather hoping not to meet anyone in spite of her firm resolve. The house was silent. No-one in the main hall — the front door was in sight, a matter of twenty yards. Voices on the stairs — Emily hesitated — she'd make a dash for it. Freedom was close, but a familiar imperious voice hauled her back.

'You . . . come back at once.' Lady Constance swooped across the hall. 'Is there no limit to your audacity? What are you doing here, girl?'

'Leaving, Madam, just as you wanted. I thought . . .'

'You thought, as my father-in-law is dead, there is nothing more to be achieved at Mountford Hall. Your brazen behaviour has failed. Death has snatched your triumph from you and now you are sneaking away . . .'

'I am not sneaking away. I am catching a train for Plymouth.'

Her heart was thumping but she walked calmly towards the front door.

'You will not. You will stay here until I say you may leave.'

'But yesterday you said . . .'

'Yesterday was different. Today, Lord Alfred is dead. Doctor Moss . . .' She turned to her companion behind her. 'I want you to witness this girl attempting to escape. You, my dear, will stay here until after the funeral, under close supervision. Lord Alfred, poor soul, was in good health yesterday . . . before you lured him out . . .'

'I wouldn't say good health,' Dr

Moss protested weakly.

'Sufficiently good to say his death is a surprise? This girl, Emily Trembarth, was the last person to see Lord Alfred alive. And she gave him his last drink, which may have caused his death! Now do you understand?'

Ignoring the shocked white faces of Emily and Dr Moss, Lady Constance rang the bell.

'Mr Williams will take you back to the servants' quarters and you must remain there. If you attempt to leave, I will have no hesitation in involving the police to make sure you are apprehended and brought back.'

Emily picked up her bag.

'I can make my own way thank you. I do not need an escort.'

That week, between Lord Alfred's death and funeral, was one of the longest and most miserable Emily had ever spent. Nobody spoke to her. Clarrie moved out of their attic, preferring to squeeze in with Martha rather than be associated with Emily

Trembarth, the outcast.

Only Sir Ralph spoke kindly to her, but his warning was a grave one.

'It's for your own good, Emily, to remain until the affair is looked into, after the funeral.'

'But what am I accused of?' Emily cried. 'I was fond of Lord Alfred.'

Sir Ralph doubted Emily had anything to do with his father's death, but his wife's fury was implacable and he had too many other problems to worry about other than the fate of a parlour maid in whom his father had taken such a strange interest.

At the end of the third day, Emily could no longer stand the isolation and idleness. She asked Mr Williams for any task which would keep her occupied. He gave her a quantity of old silver to clean, in a tiny cubby-hole well away from the main servants' hall. It was there Harry found her after he had delivered salmon for the funeral feast the following day.

She was bitter, a sense of deep

injustice gnawing at her. Harry looked at her strangely. He cleared his throat, shifted his feet.

'I'm sorry . . . ' he began.

'About Lord Alfred?'

'No — I never once even spoke to him. I'm sorry you won't come back to Treskillen.'

'But I meant to . . . then . . . then Lord Alfred died. I was going to surprise you. Do you still want me to?'

'I've asked you often enough, haven't I?'

'Not lately.'

'You've changed since you've been at this place, Emily. I was unsure. Shall I come for you after the funeral then?'

'I need to go to Plymouth first.'

'You'll let me know then?'

'I will.'

Harry looked at her mouth, kissed her cheek, and left.

Lord Alfred's funeral was a dignified and solemn affair. He was buried in the family graveyard, where countless

Mountfords had for centuries been laid to rest. Lamps in the Hall were lit by early afternoon, but it was only after the second round of sherries that the atmosphere lightened a little.

Eventually the final carriage rumbled away. Sir, or Lord Ralph as he now was, called all the staff together in the servants' hall. Emily had reluctantly been pressed into service to help serve the food and drink earlier, and she was about to slip back into her bolt-hole when she noticed Noah Templeton with Sir Ralph. His eyes sought hers and he shook his head to indicate she must not leave. So she stayed to hear the startled gasps around her as Sir Ralph spoke of his plans.

'I have decided to close Mountford Hall for the duration. Business interests in London necessitate I spend more time there and the estate will continue under the supervision of the present manager. I have instructed that as many staff as appropriate should be employed as outside estate workers.

The rest, I fear, can no longer be employed at the Hall.'

Of course, this was Lady Constance's decision. Without his father's presence to stiffen his resolve, Sir Ralph had crumbled. And death duties on the estate would be enormous. Two fully-staffed houses made no sense at all. He left it to Williams to tie up the details of the closure.

As the staff dispersed, Noah sought out Emily.

'Miss Trembarth, I'm glad to see you still here. Not at Treskillen yet?'

Emily's heart skipped. She remembered his inexplicable anger at their last meeting but he was glad to see her.

'Lady Constance insists I remain here, though I'd much prefer . . .'

'Mr Templeton . . .' Williams had come back into the hall. 'Mr Brightwell and partner want you in the library. The will is to be read.'

'Thank you, Williams.' He offered his arm to Emily. 'May I escort you to the library? Mr Brightwell is Lord

145

Alfred's London solicitor. The will was lodged in his London chambers.'

'What has Lord Alfred's will to do with me?'

'My instruction from Lord Alfred was to make sure you were present at the reading. We shall be holding up the proceedings if we don't go in now.'

Mr Williams looked so shocked, her instinct was to turn and flee, but Noah grasped her elbow and was leading her to the library.

'You're trembling. What's the matter?' he asked kindly.

'I don't want to go in there. I fear the Mountfords . . . Lady Constance!'

'There is nothing to fear,' he murmured, 'unless you've done something wrong.'

There were few people in the library but every head turned as Emily entered, amazement registering on every face except that of a short balding man who came forward to greet her.

'Miss Trembarth? Please take a seat. I am Mr Brightwell, Lord Alfred

Mountford's solicitor.'

'What is she doing here? Noah, are you out of your senses?'

'I am doing as instructed by Lord Alfred, Lady Constance. No doubt Mr Brightwell will enlighten us all . . . if you have the patience to hear him.'

Mr Brightwell looked relieved and began his reading of the legal document which passed the bulk of the Mountford Estates, entirely properly, to the only remaining heir — Sir Ralph, and any successors he and Lady Constance may produce. There were some bequests and personal effects disposed to old friends.

Emily didn't understand the legal jargon, but kept her eyes fixed to the floor, wishing she was elsewhere. Startled, she heard her name.

'Emily Trembarth, the good companion of my last weeks . . . to purchase an annuity, to be administered by Messrs Brightwell, Simpson, and Templeton.'

The sum of money was so large to Emily's ears as to be unreal. Terror invaded her body as she saw the horror in Lady Constance's face.

Mr Brightwell continued, 'In addition, Grove Park House, in the county of Cornwall, for her family to own in perpetuity, so long as there are Penroses to inhabit it. If and when the Penrose line ceases, the house reverts to Mountford heirs.'

He stopped as Lady Constance shot across the room to where Emily sat.

'It's out of the question. A common servant! Grove Park House is for gentry! She's turned the old man's brain. He was senile!' She thrust her face into Emily's. 'Why? Why should he leave anything to you unless you seduced the old man . . . you did, didn't you . . . you, a common strumpet?'

'I didn't do anything . . . ' Emily's voice shook with fear.

Sir Ralph was across the room in seconds, but Noah was before him.

'Be calm, Constance, before you do something you may regret.'

'Regret? Never! The scheming,

148

little . . . she won't get away with it. It can't be legal. He was ill . . . deranged . . . '

'Constance! That's enough,' Sir Ralph stopped her. 'You make a fool of yourself. Sit down. Let Mr Brightwell finish.'

'Perhaps Miss Trembarth may leave now,' the lawyer placated. 'There is not much more to deal with, and none of it concerns Miss Trembarth.'

Noah helped Emily to her feet and led her from the room. Outside, he held on to her arm as her knees buckled beneath her.

'Hold up, Emily.'

He put an arm round her waist and she leaned thankfully against him. He supported her to a small side parlour.

'Sit down. I'll ring for Williams, for a stiff brandy.'

'No. Please don't do that. I'm all right.'

He drew up a chair opposite her and took her hands.

'Emily, look at me — and tell me

the truth. I want to hear you say it. Had you any idea of this . . . what Lord Alfred planned?'

Emily's steady gaze never wavered, though her hands trembled in his.

'No. I had no idea at all. I don't want any money. Why did he do this?'

'Did he give you no hint? It is a considerable sum of money, and Grove Park House a valuable property.'

'He told me a strange story about our two families . . . long ago . . . but I can't be sure. I know nothing of the Penrose history.'

Her voice shook and her eyes moistened with tears. Noah drew her to him in comfort and his mouth brushed her forehead in reassurance. The door opened and they drew apart as Williams entered.

'Your young man, Harry Rosevear, has called. He's in the kitchen.'

'Miss Trembarth is upset,' Noah said. 'Please send him up here.'

9

Noah stepped forward as Harry was shown into the small parlour by a very aloof Mr Williams. He held out a welcoming hand to the visitor.

'Noah Templeton. We've met — by the Huer's Stone in the summer.'

'I remember. I've come to see when Emily's coming back to Treskillen.'

'I'd like to come right now,' Emily said fervently, wondering how she could tell Harry all that had happened.

'Circumstances have greatly changed for your . . . for Emily. I'll leave now and let her tell you. I'm going to London with Mr Brightwell — business connected with the estate, but I shall be back in a day or so. It might be best if you did go to Treskillen for a while until things calm down here.'

Once Noah had gone, Harry came to sit by Emily, and took her hand.

'What's all this about? What was he doing here with you?'

'It's awful, Harry. Now Lord Alfred's dead, the Hall's to be shut up for good and he's left me money in his will and Grove Park House . . . he's given it to us — the Penrose family, that is. Oh, I do wish he hadn't.'

'He's what?' His face was an angry crimson as he backed away from her. 'Lord Alfred Mountford left you . . . how much money?'

Falteringly she told him.

'It's for an annuity. I don't know why. Harry, don't look at me like that.'

'There's to be a reason, must be. What about his own?'

'All the estate goes to Lord Ralph. Lord Alfred seemed to think his family, way back, had done something bad to a Penrose. He died before he could explain. He said something about a letter to Mother and Aunt Maud. I've got to go and see them, but Lady Constance won't let me leave . . .'

'She can't stop you — just walk out.' The angry flush was fading but he still looked at her strangely. 'Emily, were you anything to Lord Alfred?'

Even Harry! It was too much.

'Didn't you hear me? How can you even think I'd . . . or that Lord Alfred would take advantage? If that's what you think of me, Harry Rosevear, you can go back to Treskillen on your own.'

'I did wonder why you'd never come back . . . too much at stake here, I'd say and now you'll never need to come to a poor fishing village. You'll be living a high-and-mighty life in a big house — too grand for us. Shame on you, Emily Trembarth. What would your father think of you now?'

'Just go away — how can you think of such things? I never want to see you again.'

Blinded by hot tears of anger and disappointment, Emily didn't see the hurt bewilderment in Harry's eyes. She only heard his taunts, and knew that no-one would ever believe she had not deliberately manipulated Lord Alfred into leaving what was to her, and people like Harry, a great fortune.

'I'll go, and leave you to your friend, Templeton, and your . . . money!'

Emily buried her head in her hands to shut out his words. Harry, who'd been her friend ever since she could remember, had turned against her. There was no hope left.

When she raised her head, the room was empty. She sat on as night fell outside. Eventually, she got up and made her way in the darkness to her solitary attic room. Once there she lit a stub of candle and wrote a note to her mother. She'd slip it amongst the outgoing mail first thing in the morning.

The need to see her family was painfully overwhelming. Lady Constance or no, she had to leave.

The next morning confirmed her resolution. The pointed comments made whenever she came into the servants' hall were designed to be heard.

' 'Taint natural.'

'Stands to reason she offered summat.'

Only Martha ventured to stand up for her. 'She did save his life.'

'Saved it to get her hands on his money.'

Upstairs, Lord Ralph was aware of the general dismay and discontent his bombshell had caused, but the decision had been made and he hoped for a more settled life in London. By returning to London life, he hoped Constance would be happier. Then, one day in the future, they perhaps would return to Cornwall, perhaps with family.

It pained him to be at the Hall now his father had died and the sooner it was closed up the better — and the sooner they were in London, the sooner Lady Constance would give up her ridiculous vendetta against the young parlour maid.

The day after the funeral found her set on overturning Lord Alfred's will.

'Surely, Constance, you're not continuing this persecution? As Mr Brightwell pointed out, the bequest is watertight. And the sum of money bequeathed to Emily Trembarth hardly affects us.'

'That is not the point at all. The money is irrelevant. Grove Park House is a different matter. The servant living there because of your father's foolishness will make us the butt of ridicule — especially in this county.'

'As we shall not be living in Cornwall I fail to see how that will affect us.'

'The more fool you then. I am quite determined. There are several questions unanswered about that frightful girl's conduct.'

'Not that silly notion that Emily Trembarth poisoned Father's hot milk. If you are not careful, you will end up in court — for slander!'

'Her sort wouldn't have the least idea how to set about that — and you are in danger of being as soft-headed as your father.'

Lord Ralph was weary of the whole business.

'I am going to London today. There is a great deal to do concerning the state. I shall be away several days . . . if you would like to undertake the task of closing up the Hall. And I strongly advise you to let Emily Trembarth return to her family.'

Lady Constance compressed her lips. She knew what she was going to do about the girl. A good thing he would be in London — out of the way!

'I shall start in your father's rooms. Is there anything you wish to keep?'

'No, no, I'll leave it all to you — I shall catch the early train.'

It pained Mr Williams to see the arbitrary disposal of Lord Alfred's belongings. It was as though Lady Constance wished to obliterate all traces of the former Master of Mountford Hall. Under her orders he had the room stripped, wardrobes and chests cleared of suits and clothes — and even the curtains were taken down to be cleaned and packed into trunks.

'Well done, Williams.'

Lady Constance looked around the bare room with satisfaction.

'I found this, m'lady — slipped among Lord Alfred's pillows. I don't know if it is of any importance. There is no name nor address on the wrapper and, m'lady, what am I to do with Emily Trembarth? She is anxious to leave and . . . Lady Constance! Is anything wrong?'

She looked at him blankly, then back to the letter in her hand, its blank wrapper removed.

'No. Nothing wrong. You may go. I will have a final check here.'

'M'lady . . . Emily Trembarth?'

'I shall deal with her presently. And mind — she is not to leave the Hall.'

Alone, Lady Constance sat on the deep window seat and fingered the envelope — addressed to 'Sarah and Maud Penrose — to be delivered by hand of Emily Trembarth.' Emily Trembarth! Again! Ripping open the envelope she began to read the closely-written sheets.

As she read, her colour rose. Finally, she flung it away from her in temper, scattering the pages on the floor.

'You fool,' she gritted, 'you silly, silly old fool. Why couldn't you let sleeping dogs lie? Who cares now? Ugh!'

She gathered up the sheets again and viciously shredded them into tiny pieces before sweeping them up in a newspaper. The fire-grate had been cleaned, and the newspaper and shredded letter burned fiercely for a few seconds before dying to charred specks.

The letter was proof the old man had been senile. Who in their right minds would want to revive an ancient family scandal? Who did he think would benefit? All the rubbish about putting things right! Well, she had put a stop to that — saved the family honour.

But what did the girl know? What had Lord Alfred told her? And what of this Sarah — the girl's mother — or Maud, the aunt. They could know nothing of all this or they'd have used the knowledge before. Now they'd start digging. More than ever, she must get rid of Emily Trembarth.

She made sure there was no trace of the letter, then summoned Jacob. It was imperative he remembered exactly what he'd seen on the cliff top that day. His evidence would be useful — and she'd see he had the pick of the jobs on the estate in return. That interview over, she made a telephone call to London. Her father's position as Lord Mayor gave her access to powerful people.

She spoke directly to one of the City's top police officers. And there was still enough of the day left to go for a good gallop on Firefly. She considered she'd done her duty in preserving the integrity and honour of the Mountfords — in spite of her idiot father-in-law's stupidity.

From her attic window, Emily saw

her go. It was Lady Constance's custom to ride out at least once each day and Emily had been waiting for this chance.

She picked up her bag, propped the letter addressed to Lord Ralph on the tiny mantelpiece, and walked out of the room. She'd had enough. Nothing would prevent her now. There was an afternoon train to Plymouth, and she was going to be on it.

This time she walked directly through the servants' hall, ignoring the startled looks and murmurings. Mr Williams wasn't there, but Jacob attempted to bar her way.

'Where you off to, miss? Orders are you're not to leave.'

'Whose orders? For what reason?'

'Her Ladyship's. I'll tell her.'

'Please yourself. I'm not a prisoner. I'm going and you can't stop me.'

He made a move to grasp her arm but Emily swung her bag at him.

'Don't dare. I've had enough from you. You lay a finger on me and I'll report you to the police.'

With head held high, she walked out of Mountford Hall, hoping fervently she'd never see the place again.

She reached the station just in time to see the Plymouth train chugging off into the distance.

'Next one's the evening mail train. Three hours, miss. Be dark by then. But you can wait inside. There's a good fire in the waiting-room over there.'

The cold day dragged to a close — the wait seemed interminable. Emily longed to be on the train. There were no other passengers that day. Only the station master pottered in and out, attending the fire.

'Nearly time, miss.' He popped his head round the door. 'Signal's down. I should come on to the platform now. I'm closing up when this train's through.'

'Thank you.'

Emily sprang up in relief. It was dark outside. The station light spluttered in

162

the gloom, but she could hear the train in the distance. She clutched her valise, stared into the blackness beyond and saw the lights approaching. Behind her, a horse and trap clattered into the cobbled station yard. The train drew in and a door was within reach when she felt her shoulder grasped.

She turned and a large man in police uniform pulled her back.

'Emily Trembarth?'

'Yes. Let me go please, I'm catching this train.'

'But I've to get to Plymouth. Look — my ticket.' She showed it, clutched in her gloved hand. 'What do you want?'

'I'm arresting you, Emily Trembarth, on suspicion of involvement in the death of Lord Alfred Mountford.'

Emily's protests were drowned by the screeching blast of the guard's whistle and the hiss of steam as the train slowly gathered speed on its way to Plymouth, leaving Emily on the platform — in the hands of the police.

The police sergeant felt sorry for the girl, but he'd had his orders.

'I can do you a cup of tea, miss — once you're in your cell.'

'Cell! I can't stay here. What have I done? Can't I have a lawyer? Can I send out a note — a message?'

She thought of Noah, but how would he ever know where she was?

'Not tonight, Miss.'

The arresting officer looked uncomfortable, too. All the way to Bodmin jail the girl protested innocence and appeared totally bewildered by what was happening to her.

The tiny cell was barely big enough for one. Two plank beds, one above the other, practically filled the space. A rough blanket and a hard flat pillow ensured she hardly slept that night, and by morning she'd lost heart completely. It must be Lady Constance who was responsible for her plight! Now she would be branded a common criminal.

A different policeman brought her tea, bread and a bucket of water for her ablutions. Emily began to feel anger push through her wretchedness.

'I want a lawyer,' she demanded, but the man shrugged.

'Dunno 'bout that,' he said, and slammed shut the door.

It was some hours later that the sergeant she'd seen before came to the cell

'Someone for you. I'll escort you along to the visitors' room.'

Her heart leaped. Could it possibly be Noah? but it was Harry standing in the small windowless room.

'Harry.'

'I went to the Hall — to say to you I was sorry for what I said before.'

'Oh, Harry. It's so good to see you. How did you know I was here?'

'That Jacob. Pleased as punch with himself. Said he was to give evidence against you. Saw you try to push Lord Alfred's wheel-chair over the cliff.'

'No!'

'I know. I borrowed a horse and rode over here. 'Tis a mess, Emily, but we'll get you out of it. I've been in touch with that lawyer fellow, Templeton. He's coming to see you soon as he can. Seems a decent 'un.'

He looked keenly at Emily, then nodded his head.

' 'Tis no good me asking you to marry me now — you're in love with him, aren't you?'

Emily covered her face to hide the flush on her cheeks.

'Thought as much. Don't worry. I've known for a long time you don't love me — else you'd've not stayed on at that place. Mebbe for the best, Emily. We just assumed since we were babbies, didn't we? But we've both changed — and we'll still be friends, in spite of your money.'

'I don't know what to say.'

She knew Harry was right — ever since Noah had first appeared at the Huer's Stone . . . but it was impossible. Especially now!

'Don't say anything,' she pleaded. 'I'm . . . I'm sorry. And I don't want the wretched money. I left a letter for Lord Ralph telling him so. They can't make me take it.'

She glanced up at the sergeant who'd stayed in the room with them.

'What's going to happen to me?' she asked desperately.

He shifted his feet. 'That I can't say. Depends on the evidence against you. My job's to keep you here until I'm told different. Time's up, young man. You'll have to go now.'

'I'll come again, tomorrow. And I'll send a message to your mother. We'll get you out of this between us, Emily.'

'Harry, you're the best friend I'll ever have.'

Her eyes were full of tears as he turned away.

'Tomorrow,' he said. 'Mr Templeton'll be along, too.'

'Best check before you come,' the sergeant said. 'Could be the prisoner'll have been moved on.'

'Moved on? Where?'

'London, most likely. That was what

was hinted. Seems someone in high places has got something against you. Now, lad, off you go. You've had longer than normal. Time to get the prisoner back to her cell.'

10

Harry's visit cheered Emily. She was relieved the situation between them was resolved. But as the long hours limped by, despair depressed her spirits. Except for her jailers, no-one visited her that day — or the next.

On the third day of incarceration, the station sergeant brought her a meagre breakfast. He looked curiously at her. Looked a decent enough girl in spite of all the things said about her in the newspapers.

'You're to be taken to London today. Noon train at Liskeard. Be ready to leave in an hour.'

'Please,' Emily detained him, 'can't you tell me anything? Why am I to go to London? What am I charged with? I need to see a lawyer. I know a Mr Templeton — in Exeter. Can't I send a letter?'

The sergeant shook his head.

'It's out of my hands now. Best wait until you get to London. You've caused a stir hereabouts. Newsmen gathering outside the jail.'

'What do they want? What do the papers say? Can't I see?'

'Well . . . I suppose so. Can't see the harm.' He hesitated. 'Not that you'll like what you read. Daresay what they don't know they've made up.'

Emily choked back her anger as she read in the local newspaper how 'Emily Trembarth, fisherwoman from Treskillen, had masqueraded as a parlour maid to ensnare Lord Alfred Mountford into leaving her a large fortune. Awaiting trial in Bodmin Jail . . . '

No charge was specified although there was much guarded speculation. The report implied the offence was so serious it was unlikely the Treskillen girl would have the freedom to enjoy her fortune! The papers had yesterday's date. She dropped it on the floor, dreading to think what embellishments the current edition would bring.

Later, in a state of numbed shock, she blinked into the daylight of the sombre prison yard. Accompanied by a constable, she was driven swiftly out of the back gates, and as they swung into the main road, she saw a crowd of people gathered round the front entrance to the prison.

They seemed to be milling around with no particular purpose, until a man carrying a camera spotted them, detached himself from the crowd and came running towards them. The horses gathered speed, left the pursuer behind and headed for Liskeard. Emily felt she was trapped in a nightmare which would never end. Once away from her native county who would be able to help her?

The London train was waiting at Liskeard. Thankfully the platform was empty. All the passengers were aboard, so there was no-one to witness Emily's humiliation as she was taken to an empty compartment with drawn blinds. The young constable who was to accompany her to London looked distinctly uncomfortable as he settled opposite his captive.

' 'Tis a long journey, miss. I've got a flask of tea, if you'd like a cup.'

'I would. Thank you. Can't we, please, draw up the blinds? It's awful not to see.'

'Once we're on the move. So long as no-one comes by.'

'I might not see Cornwall for a long while,' she said helplessly. I . . . '

She compressed her lips — she wasn't going to cry. She mustn't forget she was innocent. Keep that thought in her head — all the time. She wasn't a criminal . . . she'd done nothing wrong, except to stay too long at Mountford Hall. If only she'd walked away that sunlit morning, instead of turning back and seeing the smoke rising from Lord Alfred's room.

If she'd only gone on — back to Treskillen! But she hadn't, and here she was, in police custody on her way to London. She gulped the hot, sweet tea and looked out of the carriage window at the landscape sliding by. Lord Alfred had opened her eyes to places beyond her birthplace — but this wasn't how she'd envisaged leaving her native county.

Yet in spite of her terrible situation, she exclaimed in admiration as the train clanked slowly over Brunel's magnificent iron bridge spanning the River Tamar, linking Cornwall to the rest of England. She looked beyond the grey metal lattice to see the fishing boats moored below.

The familiar sight of masts and net-strewn decks brought a dreadful lump to her throat. The gently rocking fishing boats beneath her symbolised everything she'd lost — family, freedom and belief in truth and integrity.

'Sorry, miss, we're coming into Plymouth now. There'll be a lot of passengers. I'll have to draw the blinds.'

One last glimpse of the tranquil grey waters of the Tamar, and Emily was plunged into the claustrophobia of the small compartment again. The constable slid back the door.

'I'll stand outside in the corridor.'

'I'm not likely to run away,' she said caustically, feeling the London prison looming ever nearer.

'It's not that, miss. Just don't want folk coming in.' The constable looked hurt. 'I didn't think you'd like to be disturbed,' he added lamely.

'You're right. Sorry.'

She leaned back against the upholstery and closed her eyes.

'It's your job — I know it's not your fault.'

The train stopped. Emily kept her eyes closed and wondered what Plymouth station looked like, and how far away her mother and Polly were at Broomehill. Had they forgotten her, too? There was lots of hissing steam, slamming doors, shouts up and down the platform, a newsboy shouting headlines. She couldn't make out what he was saying but hoped it was nothing to do with her!

The noises died away, a whistle screeched. She imagined, behind closed lids, the guard's green flag . . . but the train didn't move. She heard footsteps outside in the corridor, voices raised — the constable's — and another! She recognised the other one — unmistakable. Her eyes shot open as the door slid back.

'Emily!'

'Noah!'

She couldn't help herself — springing up, she was in his arms, and with a sob of relief, felt their strength enfolding and protecting her. And at that moment, she knew that she loved him, and not just because he'd come to rescue her, as she was sure he had.

'Get your valise, Emily. You're getting off here.'

'You can't do that, sir.' The constable looked flustered. 'I'm taking this prisoner to London.'

'I'm pleased to say you're not.'

Noah kept Emily close to him as he thrust a document under the man's nose.

'This is an order for the release of Emily Trembarth, signed by the Commissioner of Police in London, countersigned by your local sergeant in Bodmin. I missed you there by a scant half hour.'

He spoke softly to Emily.

'I'm sorry you had to go through all this. It took more time than I thought . . . '

'You mean, I'm free?' Emily clutched Noah's arm.

'As the birds outside.'

'But . . . how?'

'Ssh. First we have to get off this train — no need to delay any longer. Constable, you can get back to Bodmin.'

The officer was still studying the documents Noah had given him.

'Well . . . I dunno. Orders were I was to deliver the prisoner up at

Paddington Police Station.'

'She's not a prisoner, and those orders are now countermanded. Now hurry, the guard'll not hold the train up much longer.' He took back one of the papers and scrawled across it. 'Here, there's a receipt for Miss Emily Trembarth — exonerates you from all responsibility. Now — move!'

The constable made up his mind. Noah Templeton was a powerfully persuasive figure. He smiled.

'Right, sir. Don't need these any longer.'

Snapping up the blinds, he lifted Emily's small valise down from the rack.

'You'll be needing this. Good luck, miss.'

'Thank you, officer. You've been very kind.'

The sweetness of Emily's smile went some way to compensate for his lost trip to the capital.

'Noah, am I really, really free? What about Lady Constance?'

'Lady Constance Mountford has made rather a spectacle of herself.'

He hailed a hansom cab in the station yard, handed her in, and as the horse clip-clopped across the cobbles, drew her into his arms and kissed her gently.

'Emily, I'm so sorry you had to suffer those days in prison, but I had to act quickly. I couldn't come to you before — I needed all the time to get you out of this mess.'

She wished he'd kiss her again. She touched his mouth shyly.

'It was horrible, but it doesn't matter now you're here.'

He bent his head and this time kissed her so thoroughly she thought she'd faint with delight. He finally put her from him and said hoarsely, 'Don't look at me so, Emily, or you will never hear the rest of it.'

She almost thought she didn't care, but injustice rankled still. She sat up and moved into the corner. He took her hand and put it to his lips.

'You have suffered a good deal of wrong — mainly from the hands of Constance Mountford. She'd been deluded and obsessed, but is not basically an evil woman. She is a terrible snob, and that class consciousness of mistaken superiority caused her to persecute you unmercifully.'

'How did you stop her?'

'I had a long and, at first, unpleasant interview with her ladyship which I would prefer to forget. In the end I enlisted Lord Ralph's assistance.'

'She accused me, Harry said, that on the cliff top I would have pushed Lord Alfred . . . '

He tightened his grip on her hand.

'Don't think about it. Jacob backed her story, but James, Lord Alfred's chauffeur, was able to tell the truth and help discredit Jacob and Lady Constance. She had put the case with such conviction to her friends in the London constabulary that they acted hastily, and without verification. They are not best pleased with her ladyship.

I think we'll find she's learned a lesson or two.'

'I didn't ever want anything from Lord Alfred.'

'I know that, and your note renouncing the legacy convinced Ralph of your innocence — but you are entitled to that money.'

'No! I don't . . .'

'Hush . . . not just for your sake, but that of your family . . . the Penroses.'

The cab stopped by an imposing hotel overlooking the sea. Noah took her inside but she hung back. The entrance hall was very grand, the ladies and gentlemen fashionably dressed.

'I'm not dressed . . .'

'Nonsense. You look . . .'

His eyes swept over her slender figure, rested on her upturned face, lingered on her flawless skin.

'You look as well as any woman here.'

A frock-coated gentleman greeted Noah effusively.

'Mr Templeton. Your guests are

here. The Harbour Suite — on the first floor.'

He snapped his fingers and a boy scuttled forward, took Emily's shabby valise and led the way up a grand, carpeted staircase.

'Noah — what's happening? What guests? I can't meet anyone . . . '

'Not just anyone.'

The boy opened a door, stood aside and Polly was the first to fling herself at her sister.

'Emily, Emily, I've missed you so much.'

There were tears in Sarah Trembarth's eyes as she embraced her elder daughter, and even Aunt Maud had to clear her throat, witnessing the joyful reunion. Will and Harry were there, too. Harry kissed Emily on the cheek.

'I couldn't get back to Bodmin as I'd promised.'

'Harry was busy on your behalf,' Noah interrupted. 'He had words with Jacob . . . '

'And one or two others,' Harry said

with satisfaction.

'I told Sarah no good would come of Emily going to Mountford Hall,' Maud put in.

'But you never gave a reason,' Sarah reproached her sister.

'I just felt it. After our May went to work there, nothing was ever the same at the farm. Jabez, Michael, May — all went off to America — never even said goodbye. I never even saw May . . . never heard of her again.'

'May? Who's May?' Sarah was puzzled.

'May — your oldest sister. We little 'uns were forbidden ever to mention her name. Dad swore something terrible'd happen if we did. 'Twas like she was dead — or worse — not even born.'

Noah took an envelope from his pocket and handed it to her.

'The truth's in there. It was with Lord Alfred's will. He wrote to you and Sarah, a letter for Emily to deliver after he died. Harry told me of it but Emily never had it. After Lord Alfred died, Lady Constance found it, read it, and destroyed it, foolishly thinking it was the only copy.'

Maud turned the envelope over and over, then passed it to Sarah.

'I can't open it.'

Sarah handed it back to her.

'I can't. I don't know what all this is about. I can't believe there was another sister. Mr Templeton, do you know?'

'I do. That letter was addressed to Lord Alfred's solicitors — a necessary insurance as it turned out!'

'I can't take it all in — all this about Emily in the papers . . . a legacy. We'd have come sooner, but Mr Templeton said to wait . . . '

'I wanted to be sure Lady Constance could not interfere. She had to be dealt with first. Then I had to check Lord Alfred's story — much of it was childhood recollection. After his wife died he came back to Mountford Hall and found a diary belonging to his mother. It told the whole story. When Emily turned up at Mountford Hall and he realised she was a Penrose, it became his mission to put right the wrong of sixty odd years ago.'

'He told me something of it,' Emily said, 'but he wasn't well, and what with the sleeping draught . . . I couldn't understand half of what he said.'

There was silence — everyone looked at Noah. Sarah put the letter on the table.

'Please, Mr Templeton, tell us.'

He sighed. 'Very well — though it gives me no pleasure to do so. It's a sad tale of broken hearts and death, snobbery and cowardice.'

He indicated a decanter of wine on a side table, and Harry began to fill glasses.

'Polly is a little young for such a story.'

Emily took her on her knee.

'She's near asleep. I'll hold her.'

'I'll be brief.' Noah took a sip of wine. 'Sixty years ago, May Penrose left the family farm in Devon to work as a parlour maid at Mountford Hall.'

Emily's eyes widened.

'But May was not yet sixteen,' Noah went on. 'She was innocent, unworldly and, even Lady Mountford's diary grudgingly admitted, very pretty. Tom Mountford, a dozen years older than Lord Alfred, was infatuated with her. I assume they fell in love — and she became pregnant. Tom at first accepted responsibility, then, coerced by his parents, denied the child was his. May's father and brothers stormed the Hall one Christmas time.'

'I know,' Emily cried, 'and Lord Alfred was there. He told me.'

'But he understood nothing at the time, and was never told. The Mountfords were . . . still are . . . a powerful force in the county. In the row between the families Jabez was shot and wounded, patched up secretly, then bundled off to America — with Michael. Lord George paid, of course, though the Mountfords still refused to accept Tom was responsible for May's baby. The Penroses were paid for their silence and Tom Mountford was instantly despatched to join the army — as far away as possible. Africa!'

'May is . . . my aunt,' Emily whispered.

'Our sister.' Maud was stony-faced.

'I never knew of her. Why didn't you tell me?' Sarah looked bewildered, accusing.

'I told you, 'twas though she'd never existed. Things were kept so close in those days, and once the older boys had gone, the farm went down and Father began to drink. I remember him as a violent man then and Mother, after Sarah was born, simply gave up and died. I brought up the little 'uns.'

'But . . . May's baby? Aunt May — did she go to America with my uncles, too?' Emily asked fearfully.

Noah shook his head.

'No. May Penrose had her baby in the workhouse. Both families disowned her totally. A week after her son's birth, she carried him to Mountford Hall to show him to his grandparents. Lord Alfred recollects a figure walking away from the Hall . . . a young girl carrying a baby . . . the dogs were set upon her . . . she ran and stumbled . . . ran again. He went outside to find her but she'd vanished.'

Noah stopped, walked to the sideboard, poured more wine. No-one said a word, nor moved a muscle. He spoke quickly, as if to rid his mouth of May Penrose's fate.

'A week later, a gardener cranked up water from the well . . . and brought up the body of a new-born infant.'

'Ermentrude! The ghost — and her baby,' Emily cried out in horror. 'My Aunt May! Poor, poor soul . . . and her poor, little boy.'

'The identity of the body was never admitted. The affair was hushed up. May's body was brought up secretly later and hastily buried. May Penrose never even had a proper Christian burial.'

'Shame, shame,' Will Broome spoke sadly.

'Shame on 'em all,' Harry spoke up,

fists clenched. 'I hope they came to bad ends — accursed.'

'Tom died in Africa of yellow fever a year later, and Lady Mountford soon after. Lord George became reclusive, and Lord Alfred, after he married Lady Sylvia, went to work abroad. So you could surmise the Hall was . . . sort of cursed.'

'I don't want their money. I hate them!'

Emily laid the sleeping Polly on a sofa and went to her mother.

'How could they . . . how could they treat her so?'

'Both families were to blame,' Noah pointed out. 'Scandal in those days was a fearful thing, especially in a close community. Even today! Lady Constance was terrified the story would be raked over.'

'It needn't be. It wouldn't do either family any good,' Maud said decisively. 'Emily, you should take the money. Your mother and Polly need it . . . and we could bury poor May decent . . . if we can find the grave.'

'That shouldn't be difficult,' Noah said, but his eyes were on Emily.

Tears ran down her cheeks, but she went to hug her aunt.

'Aunt Maud — I've been selfish. Of course, you're right. We will take the money — all of us. It wasn't meant just for me. Lord Alfred meant it for the Penrose family. I see that now. You and Uncle Will, you shouldn't have to work so hard. All you did for your . . . our family . . .'

'Well, well, no need of all that.' Maud patted Emily's shoulder. 'We'll see. There's a lot to think on, Sarah, Will, we'd best be getting back. Lodgers' teas to cook. Wake Polly up — she's too heavy to carry.'

'Mother, won't you stay?'

Sarah kissed her daughter fondly.

'I need to help Maud. She's not so young these days. I'd be glad to see her retire. Mr Templeton promised to bring you over tomorrow.'

In a flurry of farewells and embraces, the party broke up. Harry and Noah shook hands warmly and within five minutes Noah and Emily were alone.

'I should have gone with them.' She looked uncertainly at him. 'But they didn't seem to want me to.'

He laughed. 'Don't look so hurt. It was . . . pre-arranged. Why not stay here for a day or two? Plymouth's a fine city. I can show it to you. I don't have to be in Exeter for a while. You need a rest. You've suffered much.'

'I can't stay here on my own. What do you mean — pre-arranged?'

'You can do as you like. You're a rich, young woman. You can travel, be independent. I'm glad you're taking the legacy, if only for May Penrose's sake — and Lord Alfred's. It meant a good deal to him to think he could do something to make amends.'

'So much misery — caused by love. I hope Tom and May did really love each other. But Tom — how could

190

he leave her like that? It doesn't bear thinking of.'

'Don't think of it then. Think of the future. Look . . . ' He drew her to a window. 'Down there, along the promenade from the harbour, that's where the Mayflower sailed from, and later, Jabez and Michael probably. You could find your ancestors in America. Take Maud, your mother and Polly. There's another country beyond that ocean — a country of opportunity. Where shall it be Emily? America — or Cornwall?'

Her throat constricted at the thought of a future without Noah, but he was right — she could make something of her life now.

'I know where I'd like it to be,' he said softly, turning her face to his.

'Where?' She tried to speak normally.

'Neither.' He kissed her lightly. 'Or either.'

He kissed her more deeply and she clung fiercely to him, wanting him to hold her for ever. He lifted his lips from hers.

'Or Exeter . . . just so long as it's with me. Pre-arranged this was, Emily, with your family — so I could have time alone with you — so I could ask you to marry me. I love you, Emily. I knew it in my heart the first time I saw you on the Huer's Stone. I should have carried you off there and then, but there was Harry, and . . . '

'Oh, I wish you had. I wish . . . Noah, I love you so much. Of course I'll marry you. There was never anything between Harry and me — except friendship.'

She kissed him, drawing away to say reluctantly, 'Noah, dear, I would still like to be one of life's travellers for a time.'

He caressed her tenderly.

'So you shall be — but not on your own. I shall always be with you, wherever we go — in our life together.'

His kiss was full of the sweetest

promise Emily could have ever dreamed of, and she gave herself up totally to the bliss of her homecoming into Noah's arms, with the knowledge he would be at her side for ever.

THE END